I0676856

I'M YOURS

RAIN CITY TALES BOOK THREE

BRENT ARCHER

This book is a work of fiction. Names, characters, places, and incidents are products of the author's imagination. Any resemblance to actual events, locations or persons living or dead is entirely coincidental.

Copyright © 2018 by Brent Archer
ISBN: 978-1-62695-124-2
Print Edition

No part of this work may be used, stored, reproduced or transmitted without written permission from the publisher except for brief quotations for review purposes as permitted by law.

This book contains material protected under International and Federal Copyright Laws and Treaties. Any unauthorized reprint of use of this material is prohibited. No part of this book may be reproduced or transmitted in any form or by any means, electronic or mechanical, including photocopying, recording, or by any information storage and retrieval system without express written permission from the author.

Edited by Delilah Devlin
Cover Design by Nia Morgan

ALL RIGHTS RESERVED

For Greg, Elle, Delilah, Luke, Maia, Tracy,
and the Roses with love and gratitude.

Acknowledgements

Thanks to Delilah Devlin and Elle James
for the advice and support!

Author's Note

Check out Brent Archer's other stories:

Rain City Tales
The Officer's Siren (Book 1)
Past Secrets Present Danger (Book 2)
I'm Yours (Book 3)
The Wedding Weekend (Book 4)
Mitch's Men (Book 4.5)
Saving Parker (Book 5)
Song of Salvation (Book 6)
Memories of Coromandel (Book 7)
Blaze of Cortez (Book 8) – Coming in 2024

Black Rock Cult Series
Rediscovering Todd (Book 1)
Hiding Hayden (Book 2) – Coming in 2024
Dragging Marshall (Book 3) – Coming in 2025

Stand-Alone Stories
Throuple Honey

For other works by Brent Archer and release dates on upcoming new stories, visit
www.brentarcher.net

Follow and Like Brent on Facebook
and come visit his Instagram.
facebook.com/brent.archer.186
instagram.com/brent_archer_writer

CHAPTER ONE

S URVEYING HIS SUIT, Toby Hayden frowned at the soaked slacks below the line of his pea coat. Hardly how he wanted to show up to an interview, but he didn't have much choice. Though the job market had picked up, he hadn't worked in two years. Each passing day made him less employable, and he was already starting at a disadvantage.

"Damn you, Mark," he muttered. A cloud as dark and threatening as the ones in the sky descended on his mood and self-confidence.

The sidewalk lightened, and he marveled at the sudden change in the weather. Sunshine reflected off the glass, metal, and polished stone of the downtown skyscrapers. Fifteen minutes ago, a bone-chilling wind had blasted up the hill of University Street, sweeping a pelting rain sideways.

Moments before the clouds parted, a strong gust ripped between the buildings and cracked the thin, metal arms of his umbrella. With a snap, the metal broke and punched a hole in the fabric covering.

Now as the wind continued to whistle around the skyscrapers, blue sky promised at least a few minutes of respite from the February storm.

The new steel and glass building rose before him, and he did his best to shake off the excess water from his clothes. After depositing his wrecked umbrella into the trash can on the street corner and straightening his tie, he entered the lobby.

A young man perched on a stool at the concierge desk—probably mid to late twenties and the most piercing ice-blue eyes—stared through a wavy lock of black hair. The badge on his grey suit jacket identified him as Merrick.

Their gazes locked, and Toby felt compelled by an immediate attraction to approach. Though he knew what floor his interview was on, he gave into the urge to speak to this young man. "Hi, I'm looking for Herrington, Fisher, and Scallione. Do you know what floor I need?"

Merrick's face brightened into a professional smile. "Certainly, sir." He stood, towering over Toby's six-foot frame and sweeping his long arm toward the elevators. "Take the second bank to floor twenty, and it should be the third doorway along the hall on the left."

"Great, uh, thanks." Reluctant to leave, he lingered for a moment. "Are you having a good morning?"

The smile turned more genuine. "I am, thanks for asking. What brings you into the building today?"

"An interview. I'm pretty nervous." He again glanced over his suit with a frown, though his mood had vastly improved being in the young man's company. "And the wet pants won't exactly give a good first impression."

"My friends constantly tell me I'm the luckiest person

they know." Merrick stuck out his hand, a gleam in his blue eyes. "Maybe some will rub off."

Deciding he didn't have much to lose, Toby clasped the offered hand. Soft skin squeezed in a firm, but not competitive, grip. For an intense moment, all other sounds and movements disappeared in the bustling lobby. Toby's focus narrowed to the contact between them and the deep blue gaze that held steady with his.

Before releasing Merrick's hand, he gave a quick squeeze. Their fingers drifted apart, and the sounds of the city returned. Both men slowly let their arms return to their sides.

Clearing his throat, Merrick, momentarily startled, resumed his seat. He quickly recovered his smile and gave a wink. "Up the elevator to twenty. You'll do great. I'll look forward to hearing how it went."

Slightly shaken, Toby nodded his thanks and hurried to the elevator. As he waited for the lift, he shook his head. *Get it together, Tobias Hayden.*

The doors opened, and he stepped into the carriage, still unable to get the brief encounter with the concierge out of his mind. The man's smile and warmth soothed his nerves, and that handshake had been positively electrifying.

At floor twenty, the doors opened to a plush carpet and wood-paneled walls. He took a confident breath and stepped from the elevator. Following Merrick's directions, he quickly found the glass door with Herrington, Fisher, and Scallione stenciled in block letters across a frosted logo.

Inside, framed sepia-toned photographs of Seattle landmarks covered the walls of the reception area. A woman in her forties glanced up at his entry and held up a finger. She turned to her screen. "Yes, McKenzie. I have Oliver Stockton on line two. One moment." She pushed a button on the phone and returned her attention to Toby. "Can I help you?" Though a bit dour, her words carried a friendly tone.

He approached the counter. "Yes, hi. I'm here to see Mr. Herrington. I have an interview at nine."

Scanning her monitor, she nodded. "Tobias Hayden?"

"Toby, yes."

"I'll let him know you're here. Have a seat." She motioned toward three upholstered chairs sitting beneath prints of the Space Needle, Pike Place Market, and the old King Dome.

"Thanks." Giving her a cheerful smile, he stepped to the chair closest to the interior hallway and settled in. He heeded the advice he'd been given by the receptionist at his last position: Always be nice to the front desk staff. They can make or break a job prospect.

As he waited, his mind drifted back to Merrick. The bright, captivating smile and the stunning blue of his eyes burned into his thoughts. The man's height surprised him as most of the men sparking an interest in him were shorter. He started. Interest? He'd sworn off dating and wasn't about to start now. If he didn't land this job, he'd be leaving Seattle anyway.

"Ah, you must be Mr. Hayden." A slender woman with long, dark hair tied up in a bun strode into the room.

She extended her hand. "I'm Sara, Mr. Herrington's assistant."

He rose and grasped the offered hand. "A pleasure. Please, call me Toby."

"All right, Toby. Follow me." She led him down a hallway of offices enclosed by glass, most with doors wide open. A few had workers who barely glanced up as they passed by, but most were empty.

"Are folks in your office still battling the storm to get in?" Toby asked, wondering where everyone was. He saw at least thirty names on the sign in board next to the receptionist's desk.

Sara laughed. "No, the marketing team is in our new Auckland office, and a couple of the IT folks went with them."

With a nod, Toby continued to follow her. "I read about your expansion. I assume that's why you're looking for an accounting person."

"Partially. Roger just needs some help in general. Poor guy has been working weekends lately, and his fiancé would rather he spend some time at home." She showed him into a small conference room. A glass table with ten black, upholstered chairs dominated the room, and a large window looked out onto Elliott Bay. The sun glittered on the water, though dark storm clouds loomed on the horizon. A ferry chugged toward Bainbridge Island.

Toby's eyes widened. "Wow, you have quite a view up here. I suppose you can see Mount Rainier when it isn't clouded over." He looked south, but the volcano was shrouded in white haze.

"Yes. The view is quite nice, but we'll lose most of it soon." She approached the window and nodded across the street at the new office tower being constructed. "At least the water view." Her mouth tightened. "That one is supposed to be thirty-seven stories."

Toby approached the window and whistled. "It's amazing how many new buildings are going up downtown."

"Sign of the times." She turned and strode to the door. "Mr. Herrington will be with you shortly."

Flashing her his brightest grin, he nodded. "Thank you very much."

As she left the room, he returned his gaze to the scenery. The Great Wheel slowly turned on the Waterfront. Cars whizzed by on the Alaskan Way Viaduct, and he tried to imagine what this view would soon be with the planned demolition of the elevated highway. Maybe a walk along the harbor would be a nice way to wind down after the interview. His thoughts turned gloomy as he took in the clouds rolling across Elliott Bay, bringing a sheet of rain with them. *Maybe not.* A glance at his clothes gave him some reassurance. At least his pants were drying out.

"Mr. Hayden?"

A deep, confident voice brought him back to the moment. He turned to face the new arrival. "Yes, sir." Toby fought the sudden flare of nerves, attempting to stay as composed as possible.

His interviewer stood on the taller side, but not quite as tall as Toby. His presence, however, dominated the room. Graying at the temples, with silvery streaks through his dark straight hair, William Herrington's green eyes were as hard as steel and his gaze unwavering.

The senior partner of the firm fixed him with an appraising stare. "Have a seat. I apologize for my tardiness. We've been having some trouble with the accounting software we installed last week."

Moving to the chair opposite from Mr. Herrington, Toby reached across the table and shook his hand. "Nice to meet you, sir. I've heard and read a lot about your firm, and I appreciate you taking the time to interview me."

Herrington gave Toby's hand two shakes before he released it. "Not at all. I've called all three of the references you gave, and they recommended you highly. You have a degree from the University of Washington, I gather?"

"Yes. Accounting with a history minor." He opened the folder he'd managed to keep dry under his pea coat and reached for one of his resumes.

With a wave of his hand, Herrington kept his gaze firmly on Toby. "No need. I've already read it. This interview is more to discuss your qualifications and to meet you."

Sara rounded the corner and stepped into the conference room. "Mr. Herrington, sorry to interrupt."

"Yes?" He swept his gaze to her.

Toby didn't see any annoyance. A good sign from a prospective employer.

"The software froze again, and Roger is panicking."

Sighing, Herrington rolled his eyes. "I'll be there in a moment." He turned back to Toby. "If you'll excuse me, I need to calm my controller."

Leaping at the chance to show his skills and knowledge, Toby rose from his chair. "I might be able to help."

With a skeptical raise of an eyebrow, Herrington nodded. "Come take a look." He strode out the door and was followed by Sara down the hallway.

Toby scurried after them and rounded the corner as they stepped into one of the offices. There, a man held his head in his hands with his elbows on the desk in front of him. Reddish-brown locks poked out from his clenching fingers. "I just don't get why this isn't working."

Herrington patted the man's shoulder. "Take it easy. What happened?"

"I installed the upgrade and followed all the prompts. Now the damned thing is asking for permissions, but I'm logged in as the administrator. I should have total access." He shook his head. "We're going to have to uninstall and start over. Again."

Stepping into the room, Toby maneuvered around Herrington. "If I might take a look… I think I know how to fix this."

The slender man's head snapped up, revealing shrewd blue eyes weighed down by dark circles and a handsome face. "Who are you?"

Herrington tilted his head toward Toby. "This is Tobias Hayden. He's interviewing for your accounting manager position. We did promise you some help."

"Yes, you did." The man cocked his head to the side, a questioning look at his boss. "I wasn't aware of an interview today, though."

With a nod, Herrington stood by the door. "I knew you were busy, so I didn't want to interrupt you. His resume is in your inbox."

The man turned to Toby. "I'm Roger Matthews. You have some experience with this software?"

Toby examined the screen. "Yes, this is the same system my last two jobs used." He stepped forward, reached for the mouse, then paused, looking at Roger. "May I?"

Wheeling the chair back, Roger thrust a hand toward his computer. "Be my guest."

Moving in front of the monitor, Toby leaned down and grabbed the mouse, clicking through two menus. As he suspected, three boxes hadn't been checked allowing for changes to the primary settings. He clicked each box and refreshed the screen.

Stepping away from the desk, he let go of the mouse. "Give it a try now."

Scooting forward, the frustrated controller opened the window he'd been in before, this time without any error message, and moved around freely in the software. The tension drained out of his face, and he stared up at Toby. "Wow, I think you did it."

Herrington uncrossed his arms and nodded, pushing off the wall he'd been leaning against. His gaze bored into his controller's. "Yes?"

Roger met his boss's look and nodded. "Definitely."

Returning his attention to Toby, Herrington smiled. "Nice work. Let's head back to the conference room." He turned and strode from the office.

Before leaving, Toby glanced between Sara and Roger.

Both grinned at him, and Roger jerked his head toward the door. "I'm betting I'll see you later. Nice to meet you, Tobias." His voice warmed from its prior tense and frustrated tone.

Buoyed by their approval, he hurried out the door and caught up to Herrington as they entered the conference room. He resumed the seat across the table from the senior partner.

"Well, I'd say that took care of the conversation about your qualifications." Mr. Herrington absently drummed his fingers on the conference room table. "We've been working on that installation for a week, and Roger has been on the phone with support for more than half of that time. One problem after another." He shook his head. "We spent two hours troubleshooting this morning with those idiots, and then you come in, click some boxes in a hidden menu, and we're off to the races."

Toby nodded, unsure where this conversation was going. "I've been through a couple rounds of these installations. You're right that the support for the software is terrible." He thought back to the first time he'd sat in Roger's chair, beating his head against the wall while trying to make the software work. That led to thoughts about his prior job and the bitterness his sudden and swift departure had caused. He blinked his eyes to dispel the memories and refocused his attention on his interviewer.

Leaning back in the chair, Herrington laced his fingers behind his head. "With your education and references, and the practical demonstration of your skills, I feel confident in offering you the job. Salary is sixty-five a year, and I think you'll find our benefits and 401k-matching competitive."

Excitement welled inside him as he tried to remain calm. "Thank you, sir. I accept." With that salary, he could easily climb out of debt and set aside a little bit to build up his savings to buy another house. The future brightened considerably from his previous cloudy prospects.

Herrington pushed out of his chair. "Excellent. I'll inform Roger. He'll be your direct supervisor, and you both report to me. How does next week sound for a start date?"

"Perfect, sir. I have a few things to finish up before I can begin." Standing, he extended his hand.

Grasping it, Herrington gave the same two shakes. "Welcome to the firm. Oh, and dispense with the *sir*. Makes me feel old. I'm a little formal but not too stuffy. I prefer 'Mr. Herrington' when you address me, but the other two partners go by their first names. Their choice, not mine." A twitch of annoyance sparked on his face for just a moment, then was replaced with a slight smile before he moved to the door and motioned down the hall. "Sara will show you out. See you on Monday." He turned and moved away as his assistant stepped to the door.

"Did it go well?" She swept her arm to the hallway.

Toby grinned, giddy with the unexpected turn of events and his imminent employment. "I start next week."

ON MONDAY MORNING, Toby entered the Puget Sound

Plaza lobby—his suit dry and his steps confident.

"Good morning, Toby." Merrick pushed off his chair and approached. "Congrats on the new job."

"How did you know?" The concierge had been gone to lunch by the time he'd come down from the interview. Now a week later, he not only remembered Toby's name but also that he'd been interviewing.

With an appreciative smile, Merrick stepped back and looked over Toby's suit. "You're a lot happier, likely because your pants aren't soaked through, and you're back here dressed like you're ready to start work."

"I'm impressed you remember me." Toby had remembered every inch of Merrick, especially the tingles from their handshake. "Your luck certainly rubbed off."

"Oh, yeah?" Merrick cocked his head, his blue eyes sparkling.

"I quickly fixed a software issue, which impressed the big boss. He hired me on the spot," Toby said with a grin. "I owe you a drink."

Merrick crossed his arms, and a slow frown darkened his handsome face. "Are you coming on to me?"

"No…uh…I…" Toby spluttered, afraid he'd offended the guy he would undoubtedly be seeing every day as he came into work. "I just wanted to thank you for taking my mind off my nerves."

"Pity." Merrick shrugged, the corners of his lips curving up and his eyebrows wriggling. "But I'll still have that drink with you."

Eyes widening, Toby realized he'd been had and grinned. "Are you always so mischievous?"

"Only when I'm interested in someone." Merrick glanced around the lobby. "Tonight, six-thirty?"

Checking his watch, Toby nodded. He had about five minutes to get upstairs and meet his new supervisor, Roger Matthews. "If I had time now, I'd take you for a cup of coffee."

"It's okay." Merrick shrugged. "I have to get back to my chair anyway." He led Toby to his desk. "So, tonight?"

"I'm off at five. I'll check in with you before I leave. Sound good?" He gave his watch another glance. Three minutes to go. "I gotta get to the office."

"See you tonight, then. Wow, I actually have a date for Valentine's Day." Merrick wriggled his eyebrows. "How exciting."

Toby gave him a wave and hurried to the elevator before he could say something to ruin the moment. As the door closed on him and the other nine people crammed into the small car, he thought about Merrick's words. *Valentine's Day. What a crock.* The day of love had been spoiled for him years ago, something his ex, Mark, had delighted in taunting him about.

Leaving the elevator, he stepped across the threshold of the office lobby at exactly eight. The receptionist nodded as she fielded a call. Unsure where to go, Toby waited, scanning the counter as she clicked her mouse and scheduled a meeting. Front and center on the counter sat a bowl of candy hearts with Valentine's phrases. *Be Mine. I Heart You. Kiss Me. Let's Get Busy.*

He turned away, rolling his eyes. Though he wanted to make a good impression with his new coworkers, the sickly-sweet sentiments of a day of false affection roiled him. He'd always been the romantic one, and what good had it gotten him? Mark had never brought him roses or candies. The one time he'd tried to get into the spirit of the day, Mark had laughed uncomfortably and apologized, saying he had a work meeting. The liar had been running out to meet one of his several affairs during their relationship.

Footsteps behind him brought him back to the present. He turned to face his new boss, trying to shake off the anger threatening his composure.

"Good morning, Tobias." Herrington greeted him warmly. "You looked lost in thought."

"Oh, just eager to get started." He shook off the unpleasant memories. Time to get his head in a new game. Mark Spencer was not going to ruin his first day at his new job.

"That's the spirit. I meant to be out here to greet you as you came in, but I had to get the wife some flowers. I nearly forgot." He clasped his hand on Toby's shoulder. "I'd have been in the dog house if she didn't get a bouquet."

Tamping down a grimace, he nodded in what he hoped was sympathy. "So, where do we start today?"

"Well, thanks to you, Roger is finished with the software installation and no longer pulling out his hair. We need you to help with the data transfer, and then some testing." He released his grip and led the way down the hall.

Toby followed, relieved he'd managed to turn the

conversation away from the sentiments of the day. Maybe the date with the concierge this particular evening was a bad idea. Come to think of it, Seattle restaurants would be crammed full by six on Valentine's Day.

As they entered a glass-enclosed office, Herrington pulled out a chair at an empty desk. "Here's where you'll be."

The glass desk sparkled in the morning sun beaming through the wall-to-ceiling window. This office was on a different side of the building than the conference room where he'd interviewed, facing north instead of west. Still, the view included a sliver of Elliott Bay, along with a panorama of skyscrapers, including two ornate buildings that had once been theaters.

He moved to the chair and sat. His boss maneuvered around the desk and stood at the window. "We'll get you a couple of chairs. If you're missing anything, Elsibeth at the front desk should be able to order it for you." Turning, he headed for the door. "Roger will take you around later and introduce you to the team."

"Thanks, Mr. Herrington."

The boss nodded and left the room as Roger Matthews rounded the corner. "Good morning. Ready for a busy first day?"

Toby nodded. "Let's do it."

As he stood and followed Roger to his office, Toby's mind drifted to his impending date. While his excitement for getting to know the captivating man soared, the thought of being out with all the lovey-dovey couples on Valentine's Day made him consider canceling.

FIVE O'CLOCK CAME quickly, and Roger shut down his computer. "Nice job today, Toby. We got a lot done." He checked his watch. "Just enough time to get my fiancé some flowers and meet him at the restaurant for our reservation."

With a sigh, Toby stood. "Have a nice evening."

Roger arched an eyebrow. "What are you doing tonight?"

"I sort of have a date. Just drinks." He frowned. "But I hadn't realized what today was when I offered. I'm thinking of canceling."

"Valentine's Day doesn't seem to be your favorite holiday." Roger gathered the loose papers on his desk and sorted them into his organizer.

Unable to contain his frown, Toby tried to keep his tone neutral. "No, I try to avoid it."

His colleague moved around him and grabbed his coat from the hook on the door. "Life's short. I almost lost Paul a month ago, and now I celebrate even small things. Valentine's Day is a big thing. Take my advice. If you like this person, don't cancel on Valentine's Day." He slipped on the jacket then patted Toby's shoulder. "Good luck."

Toby followed him out the door and returned to his own office with another heavy sigh. He'd barely been in the room all day and hadn't eaten the lunch he'd packed. His stomach rumbled, and he wondered how he'd last until six-thirty.

Passing by, Sara stuck her head into his office. "Still here?"

He nodded, waking up his computer so he could log off. "Only for a minute. Roger just left."

"I'm off to dinner with my husband. Don't stay too late, and Happy Valentine's Day."

She scurried off with a cheerful wave as, once more, he rolled his eyes. He clicked the shut-down button and stepped away from the desk.

Ugh. Gathering his coat and scarf, he made his way out of the office and into the reception area. Elsibeth was long gone, having finished at four-thirty, but the bowl of candy hearts was still there. On impulse, he grabbed one and headed for the elevator.

As he rode the carriage down, the three others sharing the lift chatted about their evening plans. *I guess I should check and see if someplace has a reservation available.*

The doors opened to the building's lobby, and he stepped around the corner to see Merrick bent over. The long, black slacks rounded nicely over the younger man's ass. Lean muscled legs were outlined by the fabric of the skinny pant legs. After grabbing a coat and satchel from under the concierge desk, Merrick stood and slipped the sleeves of his jacket over his arms.

Butterflies fluttered in Toby's chest as he approached. He clutched the small candy in his hand, unsure why he'd picked it up, and especially, why he wanted to give it to this man.

Merrick turned and saw him. A grin spread across his lips. "Hey, there," he said brightly. "I'm finished, and if you want to go earlier, I'm free now. That is, if you don't mind going in our work clothes."

"N-no problem for me," Toby stammered. His hand shook slightly as he handed the candy heart to Merrick. "Thought you might like this, it being Valentine's Day and all."

Taking the sweet, Merrick read the words printed on the tiny heart, and his eyebrows rose. "*I'm Yours?*"

Oh shit. In his nervous state, he hadn't even thought to read the text. Heat burned across his cheeks. "Uh, sure, I can go now."

Popping the candy into his mouth, the concierge chuckled as he led the way through the lobby. "Where shall we go?"

"I was just thinking about that. We could try one of the hotels for a drink." He wracked his brain. The restaurants downtown and in Belltown would be far too expensive, especially as he was trying to dig out of two years of debt.

Merrick held the door open, and the cold wind blasted inside. "Whoa. Pretty breezy. What neighborhood did you say you lived in?"

"West Seattle." His mind brought up the restaurants along California Avenue. "If you don't mind burgers, there's a great pub in the middle of the Alaska Junction. We could probably get in there easily, and they brew their own beer." He glanced at Merrick as they fought the wind. "Do you like beer?"

He shook his head. "I'm more of a cider or wine guy. I think I know the place you're talking about, and they have a dry cider I really like."

Toby's mood brightened, happy to have the restaurant

picked. "Okay, let's do it. I drove today, so if the Viaduct is kind, we can be there in about twenty minutes."

"Sure. I'm on the bus. The Rapid Ride should be able to get me to Magnolia when we're finished." He shouldered his satchel. "Lead the way."

They battled through the strong wind and pelting rain along Fourth Avenue then around the corner on Union, ducking into the parking garage mid-block. Toby reached into his slacks pocket and retrieved the key to his blue Mini.

Merrick scooted between the car and the black SUV taking up more than the compact spot it occupied, eyeing the narrow space with a frown. "This'll be a tight squeeze."

Unlocking the door, Toby peered over the hood. "How about I pull out and give you more room to get in?"

Merrick brightened. "Thanks." He stepped from between the vehicles and stood in front of the SUV.

Toby dropped into the car and turned the key in the ignition. The Mini rumbled as he leaned to push the passenger seat all the way back. He slipped the gearshift into first, driving forward until he'd cleared the poorly parked vehicle. After stepping on the brake, he reached across and unlocked the passenger side door.

The tall concierge folded himself into the car with a grimace. "Though I love the look of these cars, they can be a bit difficult for us tall guys. Thanks for pushing the seat back." He stretched his legs forward. "Actually, this isn't bad. My knees aren't in my face."

Heat flared in Toby's mind at an image of Merrick with his knees pushed up around his ears, his lean, hairy calves stretching beyond his… He shook his head, trying to clear the image before he became too aroused and embarrassed himself.

"You okay?" Merrick's voice deepened, and his gaze swept Toby's face.

"Oh, I'm fine. Just got a drop of water down my back from my wet hair." *Thank goodness for the rain.* He drove to the entrance of the parking structure, embarrassment still flaring at his mind's inconvenient detour.

Traffic stood still, and he considered which way to turn out of the garage. A glance down Union showed a line of cars waiting on Second Avenue. Third, at this hour, was Metro busses only. Fourth seemed to be moving, so he decided surface streets were the way to go instead of the Viaduct. He pulled out into traffic and chugged up the hill, then through the light and right onto Fifth.

"So, how was your first day?" Merrick chirped, his voice full of excitement and warmth.

Toby shot him a glance. Merrick's eyes shone, his gaze intently focused. Soulful and sincere. Nothing like Mark's bored disinterest at any details of Toby's life. The attention somehow warmed his chest. He cleared his throat and turned back to the road. "Pretty good, actually. We got a lot done, though I'm hoping there won't be a quiz tomorrow on everyone's names." He tried to imagine the face of each person he'd met and match it with a name, but he failed with about half of them.

Merrick chuckled. "It's always like that at a new firm. Imagine my job. I make it a point to remember all the people I meet, especially those I think I'll see again." He rubbed his forehead. "Not easy, but it pays off. I think it brightens people's day to be remembered."

"You certainly brightened mine." Heat rushed to Toby's cheeks as the words tumbled out, but he liked Merrick's voice, the way his enthusiasm infused his every word.

"I'm glad I could help." Merrick grinned. "My evening is going pretty well so far."

The warmth Merrick conveyed brightened Toby's outlook on their date together. Even with the unwelcomed intrusion of Mark's memory, Merrick's demeanor and unwavering interest touched a part of Toby he thought he'd buried deep.

Just before they reached the International District, Toby cut down to First Avenue and turned left. The traffic moved slowly near the two stadiums, but a glance at the lower deck of the concrete Viaduct validated the choice he'd made. The southbound highway was a parking lot. After Holden Street, the traffic lightened, and they cruised along the low brick buildings of the Sodo District to the onramp for the West Seattle Bridge.

Merrick whistled. "I'd have taken the Viaduct and sat inching along forever. You really know your way around the south end of Seattle."

Toby chuckled. "Us West Seattleites have learned the hard way that the Viaduct is seldom the best choice at rush hour."

As they drove over the high bridge, wind and rain buffeted the car. The truck in front of them swerved to miss a piece of debris in the roadway, and Merrick clutched Toby's thigh as he gasped.

Toby maneuvered the car easily around the obstruction.

Merrick's hand stayed firmly clasped on Toby's thigh. "That was exciting."

Toby patted the hand, now more relaxed but still in contact with him. The light pressure and the warmth against his slacks caused a stirring farther along in his trousers, as well as more of the warmth of basking in Merrick's attention and interest.

"You're a good driver." The long fingers moved in a gentle rubbing pattern.

Shivers of pleasure traversed through his leg and into his crotch. Toby's breath caught in his throat. "Thanks."

Merrick's fingers traveled up Toby's thigh. "You have strong legs," he murmured, his voice deeper now and a little breathier.

"I run around the track three times a week. Helps with my stress." His underwear and slacks stretched, confining his rapidly expanding dick. A light moan escaped his lips, and his leg jumped.

Merrick lifted his hand and placed it back in his lap. "Sorry."

"Don't be. It felt...nice." Disappointment made him sigh as they rounded the curve and continued up the hill, passing the brown metal structure of the steel mill. He shot Merrick a quick glance. "It's been a long time since anyone touched me like that."

"Seriously?" Merrick asked, voice incredulous as he tilted his head and studied Toby's face. "One of these days

I'll give you one of my patented massages." He cracked his knuckles. "I took a full year of classes. Sometimes, I do massage on the side to supplement the concierge income." He grinned. "But I'll do you for free."

His cheeks burned again. "I'll look forward to that," Toby nearly stammered. His already hardened cock pulsed uncomfortably as he imagined those big hands running over his body, and he found he already missed the gentle pressure of Merrick's hand resting on his thigh.

Concentrating hard on the road, Toby turned from Alaska onto Forty-Second Avenue and parked the car in the public lot. Shutting off the Mini, he pocketed the keys and pushed open the door.

A gust of wind crashed against the car, and he had to hold the door with his foot, and then his knee, to get out. Clicking the lock, he let the door slam on its own and looked over the car at Merrick.

The younger man pulled his coat tighter around him. "Which way?"

"Down the stairs and through the alley to the cross-walk." He led the way along the back doors of two restaurants and a furniture store, passing a large beach mural. They turned right at the watch repair shop and hugged the brick wall, darting under awnings to keep somewhat dry.

As the light changed to "walk-all-ways," the two men sprinted across the street and under the next set of awnings. Merrick sidled up to Toby as the rain intensified.

Wriggling his eyebrows at his date, Toby led the way next to the glass windows of a newer, high-rise apartment building. The papered windows promised a down-home-style restaurant coming soon. Toby chuckled as they continued on. The sign had been there a year and a half already.

The familiar green canopy covered the recessed entryway of the pub. Thick wooden pillars framed the large window looking out onto the main business district in West Seattle. Two stained glass windows over the entryway showed Elliott Bay and Mount Rainier. Toby stepped forward and held open one of the double doors for his companion.

The greeter strode to the front, her blonde hair tied up in a bun, and she smiled as they entered. "Hey, Toby. You haven't been in for a while." She grabbed two menus from the top of the wooden divider separating the bar from the rest of the pub's tables and booths.

"Hi, Christine. I finally got a job. I haven't been able to come in for my usual lunch." On some of his darkest days over the last two years, he'd come to this pub and been cheered up and well taken care of by the staff. Comfortable and familiar, this was the right place to suffer through Valentine's Day.

"Congratulations. I know you've been pretty worried about that." She glanced at the seating plan on the podium beside her. "Lesa and Vicky will fight over you. Both are on tonight, so which one did you get last time you were in?"

It had been two weeks since he'd had his usual lunch while he'd conducted an online job search, and he couldn't remember which of the waitresses had served him last.

"Not sure, so let's go with Vicky." He'd noticed both waitresses were attentive when he'd come in, but he chuckled to himself that they fought over him.

"Gotcha." She led them along the hardwood floor to the end of a line of wooden booths. Placing the menus on the table of the last booth, she stepped back. "Have a nice dinner."

Merrick hung his dripping coat on the hook just outside the booth and slid onto the wooden bench seat. "You're popular here." His lips twitched. "I don't think I've ever had wait staff fighting over me."

Chuckling again, Toby hung his soaked jacket and took his seat. "It's not that big of a deal. Usually, they each end up bringing me part of the meal."

"Hello, dear. I haven't see you in a while." A short waitress sidled up to their table. Her black hair hung in shoulder-length curls, and she peered at them through magenta-rimmed glasses. Her gaze slid from Toby and widened, as did her grin, when she gave Merrick a long look. "Who's your friend?"

"This is Merrick," Toby replied, curious how Merrick would take the attention and scrutiny. He could almost see the wheels turning in her head. Toby, out on a date, and on Valentine's Day, no less. Fortunately, she knew of his aversion to this particular holiday, so hopefully she wouldn't say anything.

Unfazed, the young man reached out and shook her hand, his smile mirroring hers. "Pleased to meet you."

She slipped her other hand onto her hip. "So, what are you guys having for drinks? Iced tea, Toby?"

"Nah, I'll have an EB Pale Ale." He noted her raised eyebrow. "I know. Shocking."

With a shrug, she turned her attention to Merrick.

"Lucille with a lemon." He wriggled his eyebrows at Toby's curious glance.

"Okay, I'll give you a few minutes with the menu and be back." Vicky bustled to the bar.

Before Toby could ask about Merrick's drink choice, the blonde-haired Lesa strode to their table. "Hey, stranger. Great to see you again." She leaned in and lowered her voice. "You were supposed to be in my section this time."

"Next time, I promise." Toby set his elbow on the table and rested his chin on his hand. "Is it true that you and Vicky have been fighting over me?"

"You betcha." Vicky returned with their beers, setting the pints on the table in front of the two men.

With a laugh, Lesa tossed back her hair. "Well, not exactly *fighting*. Just discussing."

Glancing up from his menu, Merrick's face lit up in an excited grin. "Just like my Italian grandparents."

Lesa nodded. "Exactly. That's what my Pittsburgh family calls it."

A little lost at their conversation, Toby glanced up at the board. Luna Ham and Cheese Soup and a Red Bean and Jalapeno Stout Chili were the soups of the day.

Vicky followed his gaze. "The chili is probably too hot for you, Toby, but I think you'd like the soup."

"Okay." He'd made up his mind but looked across at Merrick. "Know what you want?"

With a nod, Merrick closed his menu. "I'll go for the Ahi tacos with a cup of the chili." He turned and fixed his gaze on Toby. "I like hot dishes."

Faltering for just a moment under the sudden scrutiny, Toby nearly forgot what he wanted to eat. He could easily lose himself in the intense blue pools of Merrick's eyes.

With a giggle, Vicky's voice splashed like cool water on his heated face. "Toby?"

"Oh, uh, yeah." He glanced at the menu even though he'd already closed it. "Bacon cheeseburger with the soup."

Lesa chuckled. "We'll leave you boys alone. Come on, Vicky."

With a grin, Vicky nodded. "I'll get your food up soon." She eyed Merrick. "But maybe not *too* soon."

As the two flirtatious waitresses turned away and attended other tables, Toby turned back to Merrick. He sat there, looking adorable as he tasted his beer. "I thought you'd go for the cider."

Merrick shrugged as he squeezed the lemon wedge against the glass. "Lucille is pretty close to cider. I like the grapefruity flavor. The lemon accentuates the tartness of the hops." He took a sip. "Perfect."

"You mentioned to Lesa that you have Italian grandparents. Is that where you get your height?" Even sitting, Toby estimated Merrick must be half a foot taller than he was.

"Yeah. My grandpa and my dad are both six-five, and I got the height gene from them. I'm six-six." He took another sip of the beer.

Toby sat back, his shoulders touching the wooden

backing of the booth. "My parents were both tall. We're officially Scottish and English, but I'm pretty sure there was a lot of Viking invader blood in the family."

"That certainly explains the blond hair," Merrick mused, his gaze scanning Toby's face. "What about the green eyes?"

"There's a sprinkling of Irish in there on Mom's side." He shifted on the bench, lifting the pint glass to his lips. The subject of his parents was a bit of a sore point, and he tried to think of something else to talk about.

"My mom's family is also Scottish." He grinned, showing off his perfect smile. "My parents are a little unconventional."

"Oh?" Toby's curiosity piqued.

He nodded. "Dad took her last name, so even though I have a lot of Italian features, I'm Merrick Giovanni *Hamilton*."

Toby nodded in approval. "A good Scottish name."

Merrick leaned back, his long legs stretching across the bottom of the table and brushing against Toby's. "Oh, sorry. That's the problem with being built like a scarecrow."

"You're hardly a scarecrow." Toby cocked his head to the side. "Do you really think that?" The contact had felt nice, even if only a bump, and Toby registered some surprise at the chink in Merrick's self-assured demeanor.

Merrick shrugged again. "Tall and thin. My stick legs make even skinny jeans look loose."

"I think you look gorgeous." Again, words tumbled out of his mouth before he could think about them.

A blush colored Merrick's face. "You're just saying that because it's Valentine's Day."

Toby took a sip of his beer and turned his gaze away as he set the glass on the table. Another sore topic. He hated this day more than any other of the year, and it made him regret making a date on this particular evening.

Merrick fidgeted with his hands. "Did I say something wrong?"

Snapping his gaze back to his date, Toby sat up straight. "No, you didn't do anything. I just hate Valentine's Day."

Merrick's dark eyebrows rose. "Really? Why?"

"Yeah." Irritation swelled as he felt the rising tide of emotion. "It's just a commercial holiday for the candy makers and florists to cash in."

Vicky returned, carrying two plates. After placing their meals in front of them, she turned to Toby. "You have everything you need?"

"Looks great," Toby replied, grateful for her timely interruption. "Merrick?"

He'd already picked up his spoon. With a grin at the waitress, Merrick nodded.

After she left them to their meal, Merrick fixed his gaze again on Toby. "I think you've rationalized your dislike of Valentine's Day with the commercial aspect, but something tells me that's not the real issue."

Toby set the burger he'd nearly taken a bite of back onto the plate. This was not a conversation he wanted to have, especially today. "And what makes you think that?" he asked, schooling his expression into what he hoped was an impassive mask.

"I don't know. Just a feeling." Merrick bit into one of the tacos. "Mmm."

Eager again to change the subject before he destroyed their date, Toby nodded at Merrick's dinner. "Like it?"

"It's really good." He placed the remainder of the taco back on the plate and took a sip of his beer. Those intense eyes surveyed Toby again.

Toby took a spoonful of soup. Vicky was right. He loved the cheesy goodness mixed with the ham, and it mercifully wasn't spicy like almost every soup and chili the pub had to offer.

Toby returned to his thoughts as he set down the spoon. Ever since his ex-lover had walked away, Toby couldn't go out on a date without thinking about the bastard. His tension was doubly worse this sappy and emotion-laden day of the year. However, he knew Merrick was curious and wasn't going to let the subject drop.

"Valentine's Day holds bad memories for me," Toby began. "I was in this horrible relationship. My boyfriend refused to do anything romantic." Noting Merrick's returned frown, Toby continued. "I really don't know why I stayed with him so long. In the end, he left me." With a snort, Toby stared at his soup. "It's amazing how much you put up with when you think you love someone," he said, his voice lowering.

"True," Merrick replied, his gaze not wavering. "But I think heartbreak is important for people to experience."

Lifting his eyes, Toby wrinkled his forehead. "Why?"

Merrick leaned forward, his chin resting on his steepled fingers. "Heartbreak helps you grow as a person. You learn how to deal with pain. I found out after Carl that I could stand on my own two feet and didn't need his support. Once I got over the breakup, I was glad not to suffer his constant judgment about everything I did."

So, they'd both had douche-bag boyfriends. Feeling a little lighter, Toby lifted his pint. "Here's to freedom from our loser exes."

With a laugh, Merrick clinked his pint with Toby's. "And to new opportunities."

CHAPTER TWO

A COUPLE DAYS after the date with Merrick, Toby found himself with a spring in his step. The world was looking up after a disastrous two years. A great new job, a lot more money, and a handsome guy who filled his thoughts. Even the occasional memory of Mark or their unhappy life together wasn't nearly so devastating. Merrick was the sunshine after a very dreary storm.

Stepping through the revolving door of the lobby, he gave a wave to Merrick, who was once again perched on his stool. Pleasure filled him as he drew nearer. "Good morning."

Merrick's smile lit up the entire room. "Hi, Toby. I know I've probably said this ten times, but I really enjoyed our dinner the other evening."

Toby paused beside his desk. "Me, too."

Merrick nibbled on his lower lip, looking adorable as he hesitated. "I was wondering... Would you like to go out this evening?"

Swelling with excitement, Toby couldn't help the grin spreading across his lips. "I'd love to."

"You're not busy, are you?" Merrick's eyebrows lifted. "I don't want to interrupt any plans you've already made."

"No, I'm free. It's been a while since I had a steady evening commitment." The last one he could think of, besides nights spent catering to Mark's every need, was a singing group he'd joined five years ago. Another set of friends he'd lost because of Mark's hasty exit.

Merrick tapped on the screen of his phone and showed the web page to Toby. "I was thinking of trying this restaurant in the ID. How does that sound?"

Taking the cell, Toby examined the website. Manoa Sunset. The address placed it near Union Street Station. He scrolled through the menu and zeroed in on the kalua-pork plate lunch.

"Wow. I'm hungry already. And they have my favorite Hawaiian dish." Toby handed back the phone. "I'd love to."

Merrick gave him a wide grin that flashed his even white teeth. "Awesome. Do you need to go back to West Seattle first, or can you go straight from work?"

"I'll meet you down here, and we can walk over if you want." With no need to be home right away, Toby was happy to spend the evening with Merrick instead of alone in his apartment.

"Okay, I'll see you at five-thirty. Have a good one." Merrick gave him a small wave, his smile genuine and not faltering.

"You, too. I'm looking forward to it." He returned the smile and headed to the elevator. Excitement for a second evening out with the handsome concierge brightened his entire outlook for the day.

When he reached his office, he discovered a large pile

of papers and notebooks crowded around the overflowing inbox on his desk. His stomach sank, and he could just imagine his evening plans crushed under the pile of paperwork.

Roger rounded the corner. "Yeah, sorry about the mountain of papers."

"What's all this?" His frown deepened. "And when is it due?"

Chuckling, Roger stepped into the room and approached the desk. "Don't worry. Most of the pile is background information. There's a project buried in there, but it's not due until the end of March."

His shoulders relaxed, and he stepped around the desk to take a look at the stack. Most of the documents were financial statements along with a few contract files.

A buzzing filled the room, and he reached into his jacket pocket to grab his cell. A sinking feeling settled in his stomach, accompanied by a bristling irritation. The face of his ex grinned from the screen.

"Do you need to get that?" Roger asked, hooking a thumb toward the door to tell him he'd leave.

Toby pressed the button at the top to stop the buzzing and angrily stabbed the *decline call* button on the screen. "Definitely not."

A crease of concern furrowed Roger's forehead. "You okay?"

Trying to regain his composure, he shook his head. "It's my former boyfriend." The cell buzzed again, and a message appeared on the screen. Toby pocketed the phone without reading it, leaving the unwelcome contact for when he was alone and could either scream or call his provider to change his cell number. *Bastard.*

Roger nodded. "I take it you and he didn't end well?" he said quietly.

"Correct." Toby closed his eyes for a moment, not wanting to rehash the pain of his abandonment. When he opened them, he saw an uncomfortable Roger edging toward the office door.

"I'll leave you to get settled in. We have a staff meeting at ten."

"Hey, sorry." Toby came back around the desk. "It was over two years ago, but he still makes me lose it."

Roger waved a hand and gave him a small smile. "Don't worry about it. I have a couple of those kind of guys in my past, too." Roger left the office.

After closing the door, Toby sat in one of the two new chairs facing the window. The message waiting on his phone seemed to burn against his side, and with an annoyed huff, he gave in and retrieved his cell from his pocket.

The message flashed across the screen:

Hey, babe, need to chat. You around?

Babe? Was he fucking kidding? Toby resisted the urge to throw the phone through the window and watch it fall twenty stories to shatter on the street. Who the hell did Mark think he was, trying to crash back into his life again?

He unlocked the phone, and his fingers flew across the glass as he typed his response.

I'm working. You have nothing to say that I want to hear. Bastard.

After hitting send, he completely powered down the

phone, not wanting to risk the chance of boiling over at Mark's predictable response. The lack of romance in their relationship had been bad enough, but being completely abandoned after the other disasters he'd endured that horrible day had cemented Toby's resolve never to speak to Mark again. Ever.

A knock broke through his fuming. Sara poked her head inside. "Hey there, sorry to bother you with your door closed. Mr. Herrington needs to see you. He's in the conference room."

He turned to face her from the chair, a frown tugging at his mouth. "Is it bad?"

She laughed. "Not at all. He wants to introduce you to the other two partners. Marsha's back from New Zealand, and Angelica was out last week."

"I'll be right there." Asked out on a date, Mark's call, the pile of paper on his desk, and now the boss wanting to see him. This morning was certainly a rollercoaster of emotions. He hadn't even had a chance to take off his coat.

After she retreated down the hallway, Toby shucked his jacket and hung it on the peg by the light switch. Rolling his shoulders back, he opened the door and hurried to the conference room.

Mr. Herrington smiled broadly as Toby entered. "Ah, Tobias. Thank you for joining us." He nodded at the two women standing across the table from him. "This is Marsha Fisher and Angelica Scallione."

Rounding the table with a warm smile, the dark-haired woman reached out to shake his hand. "Welcome to the team. Please call me Angelica. I've already heard great things about you."

The woman with straw-colored hair remained where she stood, a scowl firmly planted on her face. "Indeed. Billy, here, says you fixed Roger's problem with the software."

With a twitch of his eyebrow, and what looked like a warning glance at her, Herrington opened his mouth to speak, but Angelica cut him off.

She smiled encouragingly. "Are you settling in okay?"

Sure he was missing something, he focused on the dark-haired partner. "Uh, yes. Thank you. Roger is taking good care of me. I'm glad I can help him with the software transition."

Herrington nodded at Toby. "Why don't you tell us all about your background."

Everything he'd ever accomplished briefly flew out of his memory. Toby blinked and cleared his throat as he struggled to bring his experience into coherency. "Well, I started off in Wenatchee at a smaller orchard operation, doing their books during the summer and fall. I moved to Seattle eight years ago and finished my accounting degree." He searched for the right words to describe the nightmare the last four years had been.

Angelica nodded, her smile still genuine. "Then a stint at Teller Electronics, right?"

"Yes." Toby's gut twisted at the mention of his prior employer. He'd met Mark there, and hadn't taken his best friend's advice to avoid dating co-workers. "I was there a couple years, but it didn't work out, and now I'm here."

He forced his own smile as he peered at his superiors.

With her scowl turning to a deep frown, Marsha crossed her arms. "I know the HR manager over there. She said you were an excellent worker."

Some relief washed over him at her words, but her even tone gave away nothing of what she thought about that fact. Toby had gotten along great with the two super ladies in the HR department, and they'd tried to stick by him when the shit hit the fan. Though they understood his choice to resign, both had counseled him against it. In the end, he'd had no choice but leave.

Angelica rolled her eyes at her colleague. "Don't sound so excited, Marsha."

Marsha opened her mouth to say something further, but Herrington cut her off. "Well, Tobias. Thank you for joining us. We have a few more items of business to discuss before Marsha leaves for her offsite appointment. I'll see you this afternoon at the finance department meeting."

"Uh, thank you, sir." Toby nodded at the two women, surprised to be dismissed so quickly. "It was a pleasure to meet you both."

Marsha merely returned his nod, tapping two fingers on the table as she fixed her gaze firmly on him and retained her scowl. Something else was going on with her, but Toby couldn't figure out what, though his mind spun with possibilities. Maybe she knew more people over at Teller than just the HR staff.

With a small wave, Angelica maintained her friendly smile. "We're glad you're here."

He returned her smile. "Thanks."

Striding away from the conference room, Toby retreated to his office. *What the hell was that?* He sunk into his chair and lifted one of the tomes from the corner of his desk.

A knock at the door brought his attention to Roger.

"Hey, can I come in?"

Toby set the binder down. "Of course."

Roger entered and closed the door. Another sinking feeling hit Toby. Closed doors usually meant trouble. At least that had been his experience right before he'd been forced out at Teller.

"I understand you met Marsha."

Wary of the direction this conversation could go, Toby nodded. "And Angelica."

Roger settled into one of the chairs across from Toby. "Yeah, Angelica is really great. You'll like working with her." He sighed. "Don't be put off too much by Marsha. She's pretty intense, but her heart is in the right place."

"She doesn't seem too excited to have me here." He thought back to her words. "But she did mention she'd heard I'm a hard worker."

Chuckling, Roger sat back. "That's high praise from her. If she didn't attack right away, she must have some grudging acceptance. She ran off four other accountants before you came on board, and she went straight for the jugular on their first days."

Relief made it easier to smile. "I guess she knows the HR folks at my last job."

Roger shrugged. "I swear, she has connections all over

the city. She's well-respected in the marketing world."

Herrington hadn't specified what the two other partners did. Marketing. His stomach knotted. *She knows Mark.* Maybe he should quit now and save them the trouble of firing him.

Cocking his head to the side, Roger stared. "What's up? Your face is so long I could pole-vault with it."

Toby pinched the bridge of his nose. There was no avoiding this topic. "I think she knows my ex…and that's not a good thing. Who knows what he's told her. He can be a little…vindictive."

"Well, you've already impressed Herrington, and Angelica tends to roll her eyes at Marsha, so I wouldn't worry about it." He rose from the chair. "You'll barely see Marsha, anyway. I'll handle any accounting interactions needed between us and marketing. She knows to come to me with any issues."

Toby softened his frown. "Thanks, Roger. I appreciate it."

"How about you take a couple of hours and familiarize yourself with that pile of paper I dropped on your desk, and then we can grab some lunch." He crossed the office to the door.

Toby smiled at his supervisor. "Thanks, that sounds great."

"Glad you're here, Toby." He turned down the hall and strode away.

Sitting back in his chair, Toby surveyed the stacks on the corner of his desk then turned to stare out the window. Marsha from marketing. That sounded just as irritating as

Mark from marketing. So far, names starting in M hadn't panned out for him.

A smile tugged at his lips as his thoughts switched to Merrick and their date tonight. *Maybe not all M's are bad.*

AS THE ELEVATOR doors parted, Toby was again afforded the view of the curve of Merrick's ass as he bent over to pick up his backpack from under the concierge podium.

Toby stepped into the lobby and hung back by a corner close to the bank of elevator doors. The bent-over man pulled himself up and unzipped his backpack. He tugged off his tie and folded it neatly before placing it into the pack and closing the zipper. Turning, he snaked his long arms into the shoulder straps and tugged the pack onto his back.

His gaze fell on Toby as he adjusted one of the straps. "Oh, hi. How long have you been standing there?"

"Not long. You looked like you were intent on getting your things together, so I didn't want to interrupt." Almost the truth. He enjoyed watching Merrick's movements, something between awkward and adorable.

The tall, lanky man shuffled over to him, still adjusting the too-tight strap. "My backpack isn't cooperating this evening."

Toby closed the distance between them. "Here, let me." He pressed his fingers into the offending piece of plastic holding the strap and worked loose the twisted knot allowing the catch to release.

With a sigh, Merrick's shoulders relaxed. "Thanks.

That's much better."

"Glad I could help." With reluctance, Toby lifted his fingers away from the lean muscles of Merrick's chest. "Ready to go?"

"Sure. How was your day?" He turned toward the entrance, long strides taking him to the revolving door.

Toby trailed behind him. "Weird. I'll tell you about it at the restaurant." The odd morning introduction to the two directors still had him reeling, and he didn't want to discuss the interaction, especially with Marsha Fisher, within earshot of anyone from work. He eyed his dinner companion's back as he stepped through the doorway, uncertain if it was a good idea to even discuss his work with Merrick. The young concierge saw all the players in his office each morning and evening, and the last thing he wanted was to put Merrick into an awkward position interacting with his officemates.

Out on the street, Merrick glanced up at the sky. "No rain today, mercifully."

"Yeah. I still haven't replaced that wrecked umbrella." He ruefully thought back to the day he'd interviewed.

"What wrecked umbrella?" Merrick asked as they approached the corner.

They stopped at Fourth and Seneca, waiting for the light. Toby chuckled. "The one I trashed before coming into the building when I came to interview for the job."

"Oh, yeah. That was a windy day, wasn't it?" Merrick glanced at the light as it changed from the orange hand to the white walking person. "Our turn."

Stepping into the crosswalk, Toby glanced downhill

toward the water. "It sure—"

Tires squealed, and a hand grabbed his arm, yanking him backward. A vehicle skidded to a halt inches from him and right where he'd been walking. The woman behind the wheel of a blue SUV dropped her cell as she gripped the wheel and stared in horror through the windshield.

Merrick's arm wrapped around his chest and kept him from falling. "Shit! Toby, are you okay?"

"Y-yes," he stuttered. "I-I'm okay." With his heart pounding, the realization hit him that Merrick had just saved his life. His legs rebelled, and he stumbled while Merrick led him back to the curb.

With her eyes fixed on the road ahead, the female driver gunned the engine and sped down Seneca Street.

A moment later, a police cruiser, siren blaring, sped through the intersection and caught the SUV at the next light.

A tremor ran through Toby while Merrick held onto him. Staring at the crosswalk where he'd almost been hit, the squeal of the tires replayed in his head. He sucked in a deep breath.

"It's okay. You're safe," Merrick murmured in his ear. He gave Toby a squeeze before releasing him. "Still want to get dinner?"

A shrill whistle sounded through the air, and Toby turned down the block to see one of the officers who'd pulled over the blue SUV standing on the sidewalk and waving.

"I think we'll be delayed." Toby took a few steps on shaky legs before regaining his stride and accompanying Merrick down the block to the waiting officer.

When they reached the bottom of the incline, the tall, blond cop stood beside the SUV with his notepad out. "Sir, is this the vehicle that almost hit you?"

Toby nodded. "Don't know if she was texting or talking, but she dropped her phone when she slammed on her brakes."

"I saw her run the red light." The police officer took both Toby and Merrick's names, addresses, and phone numbers, and then handed Toby his card. "I'm Officer Jason Lynch. If you have anything further to add, please don't hesitate to give me a call or send an e-mail."

"Thanks, Officer Lynch." Toby pocketed the card. Feeling better but with nerves still frayed, he turned to Merrick. "The offer for dinner still open?"

Merrick grinned. "Sure is. How about a stiff drink first?"

"Done." He gave the SUV one last rueful glance before accompanying Merrick up the hill. "But I'm buying. The least I can do for you saving my life."

"No, Toby. I can pay for my own drink." Merrick grinned. "But that's very sweet of you."

They reached the top of the hill and waited for the light.

"I insist." Toby made sure to check both ways before heading out into the crosswalk when the light changed.

The buzzing in his pocket caught his attention. Toby fished his cell from his slacks and stared at the screen. Shaking his head, he hit the *decline* button. *Mark. Again.*

Merrick cocked his head to the side. "Who was that?"

With a frown, Toby pocketed the phone. "My ex."

CHAPTER THREE

THREE DAYS PASSED before Toby listened to the message Mark had left on his voicemail the night he'd almost been run down in the crosswalk. Thankfully, his ex hadn't made any further attempts at contact. Toby had purposefully waited until the weekend to even consider playing the voicemail. Though he'd debated whether or not just to delete the message, by Saturday afternoon, curiosity got the better of him, and he decided to play it. He perched on a chair in his small kitchen and selected first the message then the speaker button.

"Hey, babe. It's Mark. I'm guessing by the swift declining of my call that you don't want to talk to me. Well, that and texting that I'm a bastard. But please, hear me out. I've had a couple of years to think about what happened between us, and I wanted to apologize. Anyway, can you please call me? If you'd be open to seeing me, I'd like to meet in person."

Anger rose as he deleted the message. *Fucking bastard.* With his curiosity sated, he contemplated his response.

Just as he lifted his finger to poke out another angry message to Mark, the phone buzzed in his hand, and he glared at the screen. Instead of the face of his former lover, the goofy grin of his best friend, Natasha Harding, lit up the glass.

He accepted the call and held the phone to his ear. "Stazi! Where the hell have you been hiding?"

Her laughter peeled through the cell. "Nice to talk to you, too. You know very well I've been traveling."

Of course, he knew. She'd been cruising up the Yangtze River with a group of her former sorority sisters for the last three weeks, and he'd missed her terribly. "Are you finally back stateside?" He crossed his fingers, needing her pragmatism to sort through the disaster of Mark trying to barge back into his life and his conflicted feels about getting into a new relationship with Merrick. Whenever the shit hit the fan, she always came through, never making him feel less for confiding his problems.

"Sure am. I'm even back in Seattle" she chirped. "What are you up to today?"

"Seeing you," he said, his voice firm. "I have a lot to catch you up on."

"Good thing I'm downstairs," she said, laughing. "Come let me in."

Springing to his feet, happiness lightened his steps. He stepped across the room to the bar counter. "I'll buzz you in. The landlord finally fixed the callbox."

The connection ended with two beeps. He pulled the phone from his ear and checked the screen as the cell lit up with a call from the front door. He accepted the call and pressed nine to activate the lock.

Pocketing the phone, Toby hurried into the living room. As he reached the front door, two loud raps sounded through the room.

Toby flung open the door and crossed his arms.

"Three weeks in China is way too long to leave me alone." He gave her a once-over, head to toe, taking in her deep blue silk blouse, cream-colored slacks, and blue high-heeled shoes. Her green eyes sparkled, her fire-engine red lips parted in a grin, and her heart-shaped face glowed. The bun in her dark, straight hair was held in place by a pair of red chopsticks, matching her lipstick perfectly.

Stazi shook her head. "Goofball. Come here. I've missed you." She stepped inside and flung her arms around him.

Wrapping her in his embrace, he gave her a squeeze and lifted her off her feet. "I've missed you, too." *Boy, have I ever.* He hugged her again.

With a laugh, she pushed away and kicked the door closed with her foot. "I brought you a present." Her high heels clicked across the hardwood floor.

He narrowed his gaze, eying her feet. "Shoes."

"Oh, shit. Sorry." She kicked off her heels and padded across the floor in her bare feet to the couch. Sitting, she patted the cushion next to her.

With a chuckle, Toby joined her while she dug through her gargantuan leather bag. "Did you have fun?"

"We drank the boat dry." She glanced up at him with a wink. "Three times."

Giving a full-throated laugh, Toby settled back and crossed his legs. The adventures of Stazi and her sorority sisters were legendary, and tended toward epic. "I'll bet you ladies kept those stewards hopping."

She wrinkled her nose. "I think they were a little incredulous we could put away that much alcohol. The karaoke each night was a blast." She pulled a small, green box tied with a golden ribbon from the bag and handed it to him.

"What is it?" He shook the box, but nothing rattled or shifted.

She rolled her eyes. "Open it and see."

After pulling the ribbon, he lifted the lid to the box and removed the tissue packing. Inside, he found a milky-green jade coin with a square hole in the center, sitting on green velvet. The handsome pendant was strung on a thin, gold chain.

He lifted the coin, turning the cool stone over in his fingers. "Wow, this is beautiful." He examined the four Chinese characters engraved in each quadrant. "What do these mean? Do you know?"

She pointed at each symbol. "This one means happiness…this one love…luck…and long life."

His chest tightened. She always gave the most thoughtful gifts. He was lucky to have her for a friend. "Thanks, sweetie." He gave her another hug, then opened the clasp and slipped on the necklace. "How does it look?"

Smiling, she adjusted the coin to the center of his chest. "Perfect." She settled back. One dark brow arched. "Now, what all do you have to tell me?"

Feeling like he was ready to burst, he said, "You won't believe—" He shook his head. "No, wait. I think we need a glass of wine for this." He rose and strode to the kitchen where he opened the small closet next to the refrigerator and selected a bottle of zinfandel. "Zin good for you?"

"Portteus?" she called from the other room. Their

favorite Yakima Valley winery.

"Of course." He grabbed a cork screw from the drawer and opened the bottle. Setting the cork on the counter, he snagged two wine glasses from the cupboard and poured them each a generous portion. He wished he had some cheese to offer her with the wine, but with the dates with Merrick and the disruption of Mark's calls and texts, he hadn't felt like restocking.

Returning to the living room, he handed her one of the glasses, then settled in the armchair opposite of the couch and swirled the wine, wondering where to begin.

She eyed the amount of wine in her glass. "Okay, you must have a lot to tell me." She took a sip, closed her eyes for a moment, and sighed. "Perfection."

Still trying to decide where to start, he stalled by inhaling the bouquet of the wine before taking a sip and swishing the liquid in his mouth.

The tannins danced on his tongue, and he swallowed. "Mark called." The constriction along his tongue gave way to a smooth finish.

The faint creases on her forehead deepened as she frowned. "Oh?" She took another sip of her wine.

"Yeah. The jerk thinks he can simply apologize and pretend he misses me, and I'll go running back into his arms." He snorted. "He didn't give a shit about me when he was screwing three guys behind my back, and then screwed me over with his treachery and disappearing act."

Her mouth twitched. "There sure was a lot of screwing going on."

He gave a mirthless chuckle. "Too bad I wasn't getting

any of the good kind."

Her frown deepened. "What did you tell him?"

"In the text, I told him he was a bastard, and that I had nothing to say to him." He swirled the wine again. "I deleted the voicemail."

"Good for you, sweetie." She raised her glass in salute and sipped.

Frowning, he shook his head. "He's never been short of gall. Why would he contact me in the first place?"

"Maybe he genuinely feels bad. However, I'd imagine he either needs money or for you to do something for him." She narrowed her eyes. "Or both."

His mouth twisting, Toby stared at the ceiling. "The message came through on a really shitty day. I almost got hit by an SUV, and I had a weird meeting at work with a woman who knows the HR ladies at Teller."

"Uh oh." She set her glass on the small end table next to the couch. "Do you think she knows what happened?"

"Maybe. She scowled at me the whole time. I can't imagine Gloria or Emily telling her anything, though." He contemplated the ramifications of his predicament and cringed.

Stazi shook her head. "When it rains, it pours. But it sounds like you got a new job...?"

"Oh, yeah. I came to interview and ended up fixing their software. The big boss hired me on the spot." He grinned, remembering poor Roger nearly pulling his hair out over the simple fix.

"You are pretty incredible at your work." She lifted her glass from the table.

Heat warmed his cheeks, and he tried to hide the blush by taking another sip of his wine.

"Oh, come on." She leaned forward. "You know you're a talented guy. So, what else?"

"What else?" he asked, keeping his voice even.

She pointed her deep blue fingernail at his face. "Don't try to hide anything from me. I can tell there's something else." She narrowed her eyes. "I can read you like a book. That's how I knew you got fucked over at the last place before you said a word."

He darted his eyes left and right, and bit his lower lip. Playing with her, he lowered his voice conspiratorially. "Well, maybe there's one more thing…"

"Come on," she cooed. "Tell Auntie Stazi everything."

"*Auntie* Stazi?" He chuckled and paused a moment until she glared at him. "Okay, I met a guy."

Her eyes widened. "Really? What's he like?" The wicked grin on her face might have fooled someone else that she was merely excited for his dating prospects. Toby knew better.

"He's the concierge at my building. We've been out twice now, and I'm getting a good vibe off of him." He thought back to their first touch and the current that had passed between them.

"You're getting goo-goo eyes," she teased in a sing-song tone.

Shaking his head, he glared. "No. Now, come on. You know I'm not ready to date again. We've only had dinner a couple times after work."

She sighed. "Sweetie, it's been over two years. Mark

cheated on you and sucked away a lot of your self-confidence, but not everyone's like that piece of pond scum."

"I suppose." He stared at the deep red liquid in his glass. "Merrick is pretty sweet. And he did save me from the SUV." He wriggled his eyebrows. "And he's seven years younger than we are."

She laughed. "Cradle robber."

"That's rich, coming from you." He considered her last three boyfriends: Emmett the twenty-two-year-old environmentalist, Collin the twenty-seven-year-old machinist, and Tarin the Latin bombshell, who couldn't have been more than twenty-three and stared at Mark instead of attending to Stazi. Mark, of course, had taken full advantage of the situation, making Tarin the third of his affairs while he was with Toby.

She waggled her eyebrows. "Have you gotten him naked yet?"

He shook his head. "You're terrible."

"What? He's a young man, and I'm sure his sex drive is nice and high." She took a good swig of her wine.

"For goodness sake. I don't know why I tell you this stuff." His cell dinged before he could say anymore. He pulled the phone from his pocket and found a message from Merrick. A grin snaked across his lips as he read the text.

Hey, it's a beautiful day. Want to meet me at Lincoln Park for a walk on the beach?

Stazi eyed him, a smirk edging across her face. "What does lover boy want?"

He returned her gaze. "How do you know it's from

Merrick?"

"Your mood lightened considerably. You have a shit-eating grin on your face, and I have the distinct impression you're about to ditch me." She finished her wine. "Good thing I drained my glass."

He tapped out a reply. *Would love to, but have a friend over.*

The reply took only a few seconds. *More the merrier. I don't mind.* The message ended with a smile emoticon.

Toby looked up from the screen. "He said you could come along if you want."

She nearly jumped off the couch, her eyes bright and excited. "I'm in."

Chuckling, he let Merrick know they'd meet him at the park in fifteen minutes. A thumbs-up emoticon was the response.

Toby pocketed the phone and stood, taking the last sip of his wine. "Okay, slip on your heels and try to keep up."

THE SUN BLAZED brilliantly in the cool February sky, glistening on the waters of Puget Sound. Though somewhat rare for Seattle in the middle of winter, Toby knew this weather well. The February Tease before March stormed in, plummeting the temperatures back to their January levels.

He shut off the Mini's engine and turned to Stazi. "Do you remember the February of our freshman year? It actually hit eighty degrees."

She chuckled. "I thought you were crazy to leave the

dorm in shorts and a T-shirt, but you turned out to be the smart one. I was cooking in that wool sweater."

Pushing open the door, he climbed out into the sunshine and inhaled the sweet scent of the witch hazel trees on the cool breeze. "It's definitely not shorts weather today."

Stazi slammed the passenger door and joined him, hugging a sweater close. "Thanks for the loan of the fleece. I'd have frozen on this walk."

Turning toward the entrance to the park, Toby grinned at a waving Merrick. Decked out in a blue fleece, jeans, and a pair of hiking boots, he looked the quintessential Seattle native.

"There he is." Toby waved back as they headed across the parking lot.

Stazi's heels clicked on the asphalt. "He's a cutie. And tall."

They reached the grinning young man, and Stazi immediately held out her hand. "I'm Natasha, but you can call me Stazi."

Subtle as ever, his best friend was never one to shy away from meeting someone new—so she could play with him.

Merrick kissed the top of her hand, and she giggled as she eyed him from head to toe.

Toby rolled his eyes, having witnessed this innocent schoolgirl act every time he introduced her to someone he was interested in. Each flick of her eyes and the plastered smile sought to hide her assessment of his new friend. Then he'd get the full review if she hadn't found a way to destroy the guy during the introduction. However, she was invariably right. He wished he'd listened to her warning about Mark.

"It's a pleasure to meet you, Stazi. I'm Merrick." He released her hand, not breaking eye contact with her.

"I've heard so much about you, Merrick. Such a pleasure." Her voice adopted a high-pitched, saccharine quality that made Toby's teeth ache.

Merrick glanced at him with a quick raise of an eyebrow, then adopted a matching sickly-sweet tone, laced with a Southern accent. "Well now, *sugah*, Toby hasn't said a *thing* about you, but I just *know* we're gonna be the best of friends."

While Stazi's eyes widened, Toby burst out laughing. "He's rumbled you, *sugah*."

Her lips pursed for a moment, and then she chuckled, her voice returning to its usual sultry tones. "Smart boy."

"Well, thank goodness you two figured each other out so quickly," Toby grumbled. "All that artificial sweetness was about to give me a cavity."

She turned to face Toby and tilted her head toward Merrick. "I like him. Mark took forever to figure out what I was doing."

"Uh, thanks?" Merrick shifted his weight from one foot to the other.

Toby sighed. "Well, now that the preliminaries are out of the way, let's head down to the beach." Relieved the torture was over, Toby marveled at her quick assessment. She usually took a lot longer to toy with his guys, and her pronouncements were frequently blistering about their various faults. No such judgement about Merrick.

Standing between both men, Stazi linked her arms in theirs, and they strolled down the path between cedar trees. The occasional orange or white-flowered branches of the witch hazel trees hung over the path until they came to a staircase winding down the cliff. Below, the wide path hugging the beach was filled with cyclists, joggers, dog-walkers, and children, weaving their way along the ribbon of asphalt. Beyond, Blake and Vashon Islands rose out of the water, and a ferry chugged through the Sound, heading for the dock at the south end of the park.

Letting go of their arms, Stazi carefully navigated the first couple of stairs in her heels while Merrick followed closely behind. Toby paused at the top of the staircase, leaning on the railing, and took in a cleansing breath of crisp air. He loved these rare winter days. Normally, he'd be afraid it would pour rain, but the heavy clouds over the peninsula didn't seem to be heading in their direction.

"Toby, you coming?" Merrick called up to him. He and Stazi were halfway down the staircase.

With a grin, Toby bounded down the steps and joined his friends near the bottom.

Stazi still picked her way down the uneven steps. "Daydreaming?" she asked, giving him a sideways glance.

"Just making sure it wasn't going to rain on our parade." He eyed her feet. "I wouldn't want you to have to hike back up so soon after you'd made it to the bottom."

She adopted Merrick's Southern Belle accent. "Well, *sugah*, ain't you just sweet as punch?"

All three laughed as they reached the bottom of the

staircase. Merrick made to step onto the pathway, but Toby grabbed his arm and held him back just as a bicyclist going too fast whizzed by.

"Whoa, thanks." Merrick stared after the cyclist as he rounded a corner at the end of the point. "That makes us even."

Puffing out a breath, Toby shook his head. "Hardly. At most, you'd have knocked the guy off his bike. If it weren't for you, I'd be dead."

Stazi crossed her arms. "Now, boys, didn't your mothers tell you to look both ways before crossing the street?"

She widened her eyes and covered her mouth just as Toby gave her a warning glare. The last thing he wanted was to spoil the day with a conversation about his parents.

Looking from one to the other, the corner of Merrick's mouth pulled down. "What?"

Quickly changing the subject, Stazi glanced both ways before stepping out onto the walkway. "Where are we going?"

Grateful for the diversion, Toby made the decision before anything else could be said. "Let's head toward the ferry dock."

Toby eyed the clouds across the Sound. The breeze changed direction as they started out, and he feared they'd need to head back before too long. The pathway went from asphalt to dirt on the other side of the point, and Stazi would've had trouble in her heels if they'd left the pavement.

"So, Merrick, how did you meet my best friend?" Stazi clicked along, trying to keep up with their long-legged strides.

"I'm the concierge at Toby's building." Merrick's happy grin returned. "He came in soaking wet for an interview."

Toby chuckled. "He was my good luck charm. I got the job after he shook my hand." A residual memory of their handshake made his hands tingle with warmth. He glanced at Merrick, who returned his gaze with a warm smile.

Clearing her throat, Stazi caught his attention. "Should I give you boys a moment?"

With an arch of his eyebrow, Toby turned to her. "Not necessary."

Merrick shrugged. "Pity."

Before he could ask Merrick what he meant, the sky darkened further and raindrops fell slowly around them.

"We better get back to the car." Toby hurried them along the walkway to a narrow ramp leading up the cliff. "Did you bus down here, Merrick?"

"Yeah. My weather app said it wasn't supposed to rain until later this evening." He frowned. "But I guess this is Seattle, right? Weather changes every few minutes."

They reached the top of the bluff and sprinted for the parking lot as the rain thickened. Merrick and Toby reached the car first, while Stazi clicked along behind them, holding the fleece over her head.

"I can take you home," Toby said to Merrick, disappointed their outing had been cut short.

Merrick shook his head. "I wouldn't want to impose."

The rain and the wind picked up as Stazi made it to

the car. "Don't be ridiculous. He'd be happy to drive you."

Toby unlocked the door and opened it for Stazi. "Come on. Jump in, and we'll go grab something to eat at Joe's."

Trotting around the other side of the vehicle, Merrick pulled open the passenger door. "Joe's?"

Toby slipped into the driver's seat and slammed his door shut. "My favorite restaurant in West Seattle. They have a rotating menu."

Leaning forward between the two seats, Stazi rested her elbows on the backrests and crossed her arms. "I wouldn't want to be a third wheel to your evening. You could drop me back at your place, and then go out."

Merrick craned his neck around to look at her. "No, let's all go grab some happy hour. Maybe by then, the rain will have slacked off, and I can grab the C Line downtown."

Rolling his eyes, Toby put the car in gear and headed out of the parking lot, turning right on Fauntleroy. "It's no problem to take you home, Merrick."

Stazi smirked from the backseat. "Yeah, he'd *love* to take you home."

Toby fixed her with a glare through the rear-view mirror. "That's enough from the peanut gallery." He turned briefly to Merrick as they stopped for the offloading ferry traffic. "Seriously, though. I'd be happy to take you back to your place."

Merrick's lips pressed together as though he was hiding a smile. "We'll see how we do after a bite."

Chapter Four

AFTER HAPPY HOUR drinks at Joe's, Toby dropped Stazi at her car. They all huddled under an umbrella Toby had in the back of his Mini. Stazi had to move in close to both guys because of the height difference.

"It was a pleasure to meet you, Merrick." She shook his hand with a mischievous smirk. "I hope Toby sees more of you."

With a roll of his eyes, Toby crossed his arms. "He gets to see me five days a week at the office."

"Well, that's a start. Tah, dahlink." She gave Toby a quick kiss on the cheek and opened the door of her silver Corolla, staring pointedly at her best friend. "Don't let Merrick talk you out of taking him back to his place. The rain is dreadful."

Toby chuckled. "No worries."

She closed the door and started up her engine. With a wave, she drove away.

Toby gave the younger man beside him a nervous glance, fidgeting and unsure what he should do next. "So, Merrick, what did you think of Stazi?"

The younger man grinned, though he stuffed one hand in his pocket while he held the umbrella with his other. "She's fun. Quite a character."

"That's putting it mildly." Toby nodded toward the entrance of his building. "Would you like to come up for a minute before I take you home?"

Merrick thought for a moment then smiled. "Yeah, I'd love to see your place."

A flush of warmth surged through Toby as he led the way to his door. Merrick closed the umbrella while Toby fished his fob from his pocket and pressed it against the black panel beside the entrance. The light turned from red to green, and the lock clicked.

"Come on in." Toby held open the door.

Merrick stepped into the lobby. "Wow, this is pretty nice." Merrick glanced at the artwork on the wall, stopping at a painting of a clipper ship with sails billowing against a raging storm. "Appropriate for today. How long have you lived here?"

"About six months, ever since I lost my place." He frowned at the memory of the day he'd moved out of his home, closing the door to the empty house he'd worked so hard to obtain and keep. His sanctuary from the outside world, and the proof he could survive and prosper without the support of his family. The loss still hurt.

Merrick turned away from the painting to fix him with his dreamy blue eyes. "Lost?"

"Yeah." Toby led him to the elevator and pressed the button. Embarrassment burned every fiber of his being. "I couldn't make the payments after I, uh, had to leave my last job."

"I'm sorry," Merrick said, his voice soft. He reached a

tentative hand out, but the ding of the elevator interrupted the moment.

They stepped into the car, and Toby pressed the button for his floor. "It's okay. Too many bad memories at that house, anyway. At least I didn't have to move in with my mother again."

The thought of going back to his childhood home with his mother made his stomach turn. Mark's nastiness had been hard enough to endure. Adding family drama to the mix would have leveled him. No, Toby would rather be homeless and on the street than deal with another round of the punishment his mom, and that bastard boyfriend she'd finally settled on, had dealt him during high school and college years.

"I know what you mean. My parents are great, but I wouldn't want to live there again." A grin slid across Merrick's lips. "They keep trying to hook me up with guys, and none of the men they find are even remotely my type."

"What is your type?" The words slipped out before he had a chance to think. His mind couldn't seem to keep his mouth in line whenever Merrick was around. Catching his breath, he hoped Merrick would choose not to answer.

"I like guys who are self-sufficient, you know? Ones who have their shit together." Merrick tilted his head in thought.

Toby's heart sank. He definitely didn't feel like he even remotely had his life in order. Admonishing himself, he resolved to get himself under better control and stop mooning after the handsome, young concierge.

Merrick nudged his arm. "What's the frown for?"

"Oh, nothing." Toby forced a smile as the bell dinged and the door slid open.

They stepped off of the elevator, and Toby led the way down the hall. His heart began to thud inside his chest. It had been forever since he'd invited a man into his home. *Stop it, Tobias. Keep your resolve.* He inserted his key into the lock and turned it, opening the door.

Merrick paused at the threshold, blinked, and then turned to Toby with a blush coloring his cheeks. "Just for the record, you are totally my type."

While Toby stood stock-still trying to find a response, Merrick stepped into the apartment.

Toby followed, still struck dumb that this gorgeous young man would be attracted to someone like him. Maybe the connection he'd felt at their first handshake was a mutual feeling. He felt his resolve, and the walls he'd erected around his heart, crumbling.

"Tour?" Merrick chirped, glancing over his shoulder and giving Toby a smile.

Toby snapped out of his daze. "Oh, right." He swept out his arm. "We have the living room here, kitchen through the doorway to the left, and a hallway leading to the single bedroom." As soon as he said the word bedroom, heat crept up his neck.

A grin tugged at Merrick's lips. "Maybe a little premature to see the bedroom just yet, but I'd love to see your kitchen."

With a nervous chuckle, Toby led the way to the kitchen. He'd like nothing better than to show Merrick his bedroom. Still, Merrick was someone from work, and he'd made that mistake with his ex. The walls strengthened again around his heart.

As if on cue, his cell buzzed. Glancing at the screen, Toby felt his face fall as Mark stared back at him. Making a mental note to delete Mark's profile picture from his contact list, he declined the call and quelled the familiar impulse to throw the cell across the room.

"What's wrong?" Merrick stood by his side, forehead furrowed in concern.

"My ex-boyfriend has been trying to talk to me," he muttered.

Merrick crossed his arms. "You don't want to deal with an idiot like that."

Toby arched an eyebrow. "Why do you say he's an idiot?"

"He must be." Merrick sniffed. "He let you go."

Warmth flared across his face, and Toby struggled to meet Merrick's gaze. "I'm not all that and a bag of chips," he said, his voice going raspy.

"Look at me." Merrick cupped Toby's chin and raised it until their gazes met.

Those pools of pure blue captured Toby's complete attention. "Yes?" Toby breathed.

Kindness, and something that smacked of adoration, flashed across Merrick's face. "You've had your heart broken, and yet, you stood back up," he said, his voice soft. "I don't know for sure, but it feels like he knocked you down pretty hard before he walked away. Do you have any idea how amazing you are?"

"I'm not—"

"Stop." Gently but firmly, Merrick held Toby's chin in place. "You're one of the most handsome men I've ever met, and certainly the most together. Your strength and ability to deal with adversity is super sexy."

A quiver worked its way down Toby's spine. "Merrick, that's really sweet of you to say." Toby stepped back, reluctantly breaking eye contact and retreating from the soft touch of Merrick's fingers against his chin. "I'm just not ready for anything serious."

"How do you know that?" Merrick asked, standing still but in more of a curious than angry or disappointed stance.

Toby stared at Merrick then turned away. "You're right. Mark hurt me bad. My parents, too. At this point, Stazi is about the only person who's stuck by me, and I'm afraid to trust people."

Nodding, Merrick ran an appraising glance over Toby, like he was planning a complete make-over on one of those reality TV shows. "I know exactly what you need, handsome man." His tone deepened, and his gaze intensified as he pronounced the verdict of his deliberation. "Wooing."

With a confused shake of his head, Toby refocused on the tall man staring at him. "What?"

Merrick's gaze remained steady. "Wooing. Definitely some romancing. Possibly some other stuff." He winked. "But first thing's first. Wooing."

"Nobody has *wooed* me before," Toby mused. Mark had always been a dick about the romantic stuff. His few compliments were always back-handed. *Why the hell did I stay with him so long?*

Merrick stepped into the living room and made for the door. His demeanor wasn't one of a man trying to escape, or even one upset by Toby's rejection, but more like he was eager to get started on a new project. "I'll call you later. I have some planning to do." He stopped at the door then turned and strode back to Toby. "Can I at least give you a hug?"

Dumbfounded, Toby slowly nodded, still unsure what was happening here.

Merrick leaned his tall frame forward and wrapped his long arms around Toby, turning his face into Toby's neck and planting a kiss against his skin.

Sparks flew as their bodies connected, the sensations overwhelming and exciting after so long without anyone even remotely taking an interest in him. The warmth and tenderness of Merrick's embrace, coupled with the security of the way he held his body, made his resistance to Merrick's advances threaten to crumble away. Something between a moan and a whimper escaped his lips before he could stifle the sound.

Merrick pulled away. "Sorry about kissing you without asking. I couldn't resist."

Toby cleared his throat. "No problem," he choked out, swaying slightly before getting his footing again.

"See ya." Merrick smiled brightly and headed out of the apartment, softly shutting the front door.

Coming to his senses, Toby scrambled for his keys and jacket. He flung open the door and chased after Merrick.

"Hey, wait! I said I'd take you home."

TOBY STRODE INTO the office building Monday morning with a smile on his lips and a spring in his step. *It's becoming a habit,* he mused ruefully. He approached Merrick, who shared his smile, and stood in front of the concierge desk.

"Good morning, Toby. How was your weekend?"

"On Saturday, I had a great walk on the beach with a couple friends and a rather unexpected afternoon." Toby chuckled. "And how was your Sunday?"

"Great." The smile morphed into a sly grin. "I did some planning."

Before Toby could say another word, footsteps approached behind him.

"Hey, Toby."

The familiar voice wiped the smile off of Toby's face as he slowly turned around. He stared dumbfounded at his traitorous ex. "What the fuck are you doing here?"

Mark stepped forward, his arms spread wide, but Toby held up his hand and stepped back. The last thing he wanted, especially in front of Merrick, was to touch or be touched by his ex-boyfriend.

His face screwing up in confusion, Mark stepped back and dropped his arms. "What's the matter?"

"Seriously?" Toby fought to keep his voice level, but the rising anger and confusion at Mark's presence tested his patience. "Run along, Mark. I'm speaking with Merrick."

Mark's gaze touched on Merrick, but quickly returned to Toby. "I wanted to apologize."

Toby held up his hand again. "Save it. I have to get to work, and I really don't want to hear anything you have to say."

Pouting with disappointment, Mark took a step closer. "Come on, Tobes."

"Don't you *dare* call me that ever again." Turning his back on his ex, Toby frowned at Merrick. "Sorry. We'll chat later."

With a professional smile but eyes filled with concern, Merrick gave Toby a quick wave. "Have a great day."

"You, too." He strode to the elevator, not giving Mark a second glance. The door opened, and he quickly stepped into the car with three other folks. As the door closed, he leaned against the wall and breathed a sigh. How did Mark know where he worked? *Fuck me.*

Once the car arrived on the twentieth floor, he stepped off the elevator and strode across the hall and into the reception area of his office.

Elsibeth glanced up as he marked himself in on the board and gave him a quick wave. "Good morning, Toby."

"Morning." He continued to his office, not wanting to get into a conversation after the jolt he'd experienced in the lobby. He dropped his pack on the floor. After hanging his coat on the hook behind the door, he plopped into his chair and ran his hands over his face.

Mark's appearance at his workplace gave him pause. How the hell had his ex figured out where to find him? Toby had been careful not to give out details to their mutual acquaintances, or as he'd found out months ago, *Mark's* friends. Stazi wouldn't have breathed a word. She'd be more likely to deck Mark than give out any information.

Roger stuck his head inside his office. "Morning, Toby. How was the weekend?"

Forcing a smile, Toby looked up. "It was great. I met up with some friends on Saturday. How about you?"

His supervisor positively beamed. "My fiancé took me over to Poulsbo to this awesome little bed and breakfast. We had a blast exploring that part of the peninsula."

"It's been a while since I've been over there, but I remember some good food in Poulsbo." The last adventure to the peninsula had involved a long hike into Olympic National Park with Stazi and three of their college friends. It had been one of the best weekends he'd had when his life was less complicated. Part of the "pre-Mark" years.

"Paul is quite the romantic, especially after his stint in the hospital and rehab." The glow about Roger brightened as he spoke about his fiancé.

Toby frowned. "Did he have some sort of accident?"

Roger nodded. "He's a police officer. He and his partner were responding to a call. When they pulled up, some guy was beating his girlfriend and threatening her with a gun. He shot Paul twice before Jason returned fire."

With eyes widening, Toby stood. "Oh my God."

Roger visibly shivered. "I know. Scared the hell out of me. Herrington was amazing, as was everyone else here at the office. Paul's okay, though he still can't exert himself very much."

"How long ago was that?"

"About two months. He's back at work, but he's stuck with a desk job for a while." Roger grinned. "I like it because I know he's safe, but he's going a little stir-crazy. He's not a desk-work kind of guy."

The card from the police officer who'd caught the woman in the SUV came to his mind. "Did you say his partner's name is Jason?"

Roger nodded. "Why?"

Toby fished in his pocket for his wallet and retrieved the cop's card. "It's not Jason Lynch, is it?"

Nodding, Roger peered at him curiously. "You have his card?"

"He took my statement after a woman in a large SUV nearly mowed me down in a crosswalk last week." Pocketing his wallet and the card, Toby was about to tell the story of Merrick saving his life when their boss passed the window outside Toby's office.

Herrington approached the door and addressed them both in a short, clipped tone. "Good morning. We have an impromptu staff meeting in about ten minutes. Marsha has hired a new marketing person, and she'd like you all to meet him." The words spat out of his mouth like they had a foul flavor.

Wrinkling his brow, Roger turned to Herrington. "Really? I didn't know we had a position open."

"We didn't." Herrington's mouth tightened. "But I guess she knew him from one of her many contacts and hired him to help with the Covington project. It's a probationary position to see if he works out for permanent employment. She'll get you the paperwork to set him up on payroll."

Roger nodded. "Where is the new guy sitting?"

"The office next to Tobias is vacant, so she insisted he be in there for now." Herrington checked his watch. "I'll see you in the conference room." He strode away.

Roger turned back to Toby. "This is rather spur-of-the-moment. I guess when you're one of the partners, you can do whatever you want. Doesn't look good to the rest of the staff, though."

With a shrug, Toby powered up his computer. "Pretty wild. Want me to set up the new guy in payroll?"

"If you wouldn't mind. I've got more of the conversion to work on. You can help me out with that until we get the paperwork." Roger glanced at the clock on the wall. "Shall we?"

Toby stood and followed his supervisor to the conference room. The moment he stepped inside, his blood froze.

With a smirk on her face, Marsha crossed her arms. "Ah, Tobias. I'm sure I don't have to introduce Mark Spencer to you."

CHAPTER FIVE

TOBY BURNED WITH fury as he sank into his office chair and stared at Mark's employment paperwork centered on his desk. *That fucking bitch knew exactly what she was doing.*

A tentative knock brought his attention to the entrance of his office.

Roger stepped inside and shut the door. "What's going on?" His forehead creased in concern.

Tight-lipped and seething, Toby could barely utter an explanation. "That's my ex," he ground out.

"Holy shit." Roger crossed to one of the chairs in front of Toby's desk and sat down. "Is this going to be a problem?"

Toby rubbed a hand over his face. He drew a deep breath, trying to get his pounding heart to slow. "I really don't know what I'm going to do. Mark was a disaster. We didn't end well." He needed this job. Desperately. He liked his supervisor, boss, and coworkers. But with Mark in the office next door…

Roger leaned forward, a frown darkening his eyes. "Let me make this very clear. I'll fight to keep you here. This Spencer guy is temporary, and I'll talk to Herrington about making sure his position *is* temporary." His gaze locked with Toby's. "Don't worry about anything. I'll run as much interference as I can, and we'll see about moving you to another office."

Toby sighed deeply, trying to keep a rational grip on his thoughts. "I appreciate it, but I have a lot of baggage with that guy, and I didn't want to bring it to this new job."

"Just bear with me, Toby. I'll do the best I can to fix this." He sat back. "The partners must already know about you and Spencer. Marsha was too smug. And you saw Angelica's face when Marsha introduced him. She was just about as angry as you are. Herrington hides things pretty well, but she's an open book."

Roger was right. The third partner had fumed behind Mark's chair as she stood with the management team, and Herrington had worn a frown chiseled into his stone-faced façade throughout the introduction.

Toby wouldn't want to be anywhere near the next partners' meeting.

Seeing movement out of the corner of his eye, Toby glanced out the glass by the door of his office to see Marsha walking by. She stared inside, the same smirk on her face as before. The marketing team at his last job must have said something to her, so she'd hired Mark to force Toby to quit. *I wonder if Mark knows he's being used.*

He set his jaw and returned his attention to Roger. "Okay, here's the deal. I'll stay, but Mark needs to be kept far away from me. No projects with Marketing—no matter what Marsha says. I've already lost a lot because of that shithead, and I'm not losing anything more."

Roger took a deep breath and nodded. "That's the spirit. Come help me with the integration work. If we can get this phase done before lunch, you can take the rest of the day off with pay."

"Are you sure?" Toby shifted in his seat. "I don't want to get you in trouble with Herrington."

"I don't want to lose you as an employee." Roger stood and headed to the door. "Hopefully tomorrow, I'll have you moved into another spot on the far side of the floor. Get something to drink and join me in my office."

Toby rose, gratitude swelling inside his chest. He hadn't expected such strong support from his supervisor, being so new to the firm. "Thanks, Roger."

"I'm sorry this happened. Hang in there." Roger opened the door and was gone.

Toby grabbed his cup and strode around the desk, only to be cut off by Mark, who suddenly appeared at the doorway of his office.

"May I come in?" Mark at least had enough decency to look hesitant, though not enough to keep from blocking the door with his arm.

Forcing his expression into a neutral mask, Toby said, "I'm off to a meeting." He made to push past Mark, but his ex refused to budge, keeping his arm outstretched across the doorframe.

Mark's hesitancy fell away, and his voice rose in frustration to a whiney pitch Toby remembered well. "Can I just talk to you for a minute? I've been trying to call you."

Tightlipped, Toby's anger threatened to explode.

Spoiled brat. Mark only whined like that when he wasn't getting his way. "No. I'm going to be late, and I know you remember I *don't* like to be late."

With a nervous chuckle, Mark nodded. "I just want to say—"

"Save it," Toby barked and glared pointedly at the arm barring his way.

Frowning, Mark stepped aside and removed his hand from the doorframe.

Toby edged past him, careful not to touch him in any way, and then hurried down the hall toward the break-room.

"Rotten piece of shit," Toby muttered under his breath as he stormed to the coffee machine and poured himself a cup. Thankfully, no one was in the room to face his wrath. He could easily get himself fired, and that was one outcome he refused to let happen.

He stalked back into the hallway and wound his way to Roger's door. Before entering, he struggled to calm himself and took a deep breath. He forced his focus to shift to working on the software integration instead of steaming about Mark.

Looking up from his computer, Roger greeted him. "Hey, come on in and shut the door. It'll give us some privacy."

After closing the door, Toby brought his mug over to Roger's desk and set it on the tabletop. "What have you got?"

THE ELEVATOR DOOR opened onto the lobby, and Toby beat a hasty retreat from the car. He spied Merrick pushing up from his chair, and the relief concierge taking his place.

Toby hurried over to him. "Can I take you to lunch?"

Merrick's quick smile faded. "What's wrong? Is it that guy who interrupted us this morning?"

"Yeah." He glanced back at the elevators, fearful Mark would chase after him wanting to continue the conversation Toby had cut off. "Can we get out of here?"

"Sure." Merrick turned to the concierge station. "I'll be back at one, Shawn."

The gruff older man shrugged. "Take your time."

With his standard grin, Merrick swept his arm toward the door. "I'm all yours. Let's go."

Toby hurried them out the front door and down the street. Though flustered, he made sure to look both ways before stepping into the crosswalk. They continued down the hill and got two blocks away from the building before Merrick grabbed his shoulder and pulled him to a halt.

"Hey, slow up," Merrick said, his tone chiding. "Toby, what's going on? You have this huge scowl on your handsome face."

Toby took a breath and turned to meet Merrick's concerned gaze. "Marsha just hired my ex-boyfriend for the marketing team."

Merrick's frown deepened. "You're not still interested in him, are you?"

Caught off guard at his friend's question, Toby shook his head. "Definitely not."

"Then what's the problem?" Merrick's soothing voice helped calm Toby's frantic nerves. "You're both adults. With you being in accounting and him in marketing, I don't think there's much need for the two of you to work on any projects together."

Toby puffed out a breath. "He keeps trying to talk to me. Roger gave me the rest of the day off while he tries to figure out how to solve this issue."

"Want a hug?" Merrick opened his arms.

Sighing his relief, Toby said, "Please." He stepped into the embrace, warmth encircling him. "This feels nice."

With a squeeze, Merrick kissed the top of his head. "Consider this a bonus—just a taste of the wooing I promised you."

Shaking with laughter that was amplified by frazzled nerves, Toby released all the pent-up shock and frustration from the morning. "You're amazing," he said, resting his cheek against Merrick's solid chest.

Merrick kissed the top of his head again. "All part of the friendly service. Let's go grab some lunch." Merrick released his hold.

With reluctance, Toby stepped away from Merrick, and they continued down Third Avenue at a more reasonable pace. Walking together felt right. Toby glanced to his side to see Merrick smiling back, and he fought the temptation to hold Merrick's hand. They reached the corner and ducked into a small sandwich shop.

Merrick shot him a sideways glance as they stared at the menu. "Roast beef on sourdough, light on the horseradish, right?"

With his eyes widening, Toby turned to stare. "How do you know my favorite?"

His friend touched his index finger to the side of his nose. "I have my sources." He nodded toward the window. "How about you go snag that seat while I order."

Toby fished in his pocket for his wallet. "Here, I've got a twenty."

Before he could open his billfold, Merrick held up a hand. "I'll get it, and you can get happy hour this evening."

Standing there with his wallet open, Toby arched an eyebrow. "Happy hour?"

"Unless you have other plans..." Merrick's frown reappeared. "Do you have other plans?"

"No, I don't." Toby closed his wallet and shoved it back into the front pocket of his pants. "I'd love to go out with you."

"Snag a table, and we can discuss it." Merrick stepped forward in the line and addressed the cashier. "Hi, there."

Toby wove his way around the tables and sat down at the corner window spot. He glanced outside in time to see Mark stroll by with Marsha. Fighting the urge to hide under the table, Toby pulled out his cell phone and sent a quick text to Stazi. *Shit day. Mark is working at my new job now.*

Almost immediately, his cell dinged. *Holy fuck! How?*

He tapped at the glass screen. *Mkt Dir is evil. Merrick took me to lunch.*

Aw! A smiley-faced emoticon sprang onto the text message with little hearts circling it.

Knock it off. He added an emoticon with its eyes

squeezed shut and sticking out its tongue and pressed send just as Merrick approached the table.

"Who's that?" He slid his long frame onto the seat and handed Toby an iced tea.

"Stazi." He stared at the drink. "I forgot to tell you what I drink here."

"Just a squeeze of lemon and no sugar." He winked.

"How did you know?" The phone's ding distracted him, and he glanced at the screen.

Srsly, don't be an idiot. Forget Mark! Go for it w/ Merrick.

Rolling his eyes, he pocketed his cell and turned his focus back to his dining companion. "Sorry, she's being a little bossy."

"I have to be careful of the time, but if you'd like to talk about the whole Mark-thing, we could get a start." He took a sip of his water.

Toby dragged in a deep breath. "Okay. If we're going to be friends, you should know anyway."

Merrick tilted his head to the side. "Is it that bad?"

"It shouldn't be." Toby gave a mirthless laugh. "Mark and I met at work. He's handsome, as I'm sure you noticed."

Merrick shrugged. "Not to me. I can tell he's not my type."

A flush of heat spread across Toby's cheeks, side-tracked for a moment by the implication of Merrick's words. "Well, unfortunately, I fell hard. We were together about three years. Anyway, at the job, I worked hard, stayed late at night, back early in the morning. I left the extra mile in the dust."

"That's probably why Mr. Herrington hired you."

Their sandwiches showed up, and Merrick thanked the waitress.

Toby glanced at the sandwich then brought his gaze back to Merrick. "This is perfect. Still not going to tell me how you know my favorite sandwich?"

"Someday. Continue your story." He took a bite of his turkey with bacon and avocado on rye.

Toby made note of the sandwich choice. "Well, one day I show up for work after a couple days off, and the boss pulls me into the office." He cringed at the memory of Paul Beck's disappointed glare. "Apparently, I had logged into the bank over the weekend and moved some money into an illegal holding account. The bank was able to pull the money back, but the damage was done."

Merrick set his sandwich back onto the plastic tray. "I can't imagine you ever doing something like that."

Just as he had on that horrible day, Toby felt as though time stood still. His stomach knotted. "The thing was, I didn't. I insisted on my innocence. Unfortunately, Mark was my only witness to being home during the weekend, and he wouldn't vouch for me, claiming there were several hours where I could have been away and done the deed."

With a shake of his head, Merrick leaned forward. "I did tell you he's an idiot, right?"

"Yeah, you did." A ghost of a smile tugged at the corners of Toby's mouth.

"This just enforces my opinion." Merrick nodded. "Go on."

Another sigh escaped as he leaned back in the chair.

"Because there was some doubt, and the upper echelon didn't want a scandal, they agreed not to prosecute as long as I quit and didn't try to claim unemployment."

Merrick's frown deepened into a scowl. "And Mark?"

Toby snorted. "His stuff was already moved out of my house before I got home." His anger flared for a moment, but he kept it under control. "And so was some of my stuff. The bastard took my grandmother's kitchen table and my favorite rocking chair."

"Scumbag." He took another sip of water. "I'm guessing word got out about the situation at your former firm."

Toby nodded. "Quietly, but yeah. I couldn't find another position. Couldn't even get an interview to explain what had happened." Cold bitterness settled over him. "I lost nearly every friend I thought I had. Eventually, I couldn't make my mortgage payments and had to let my house go in a short sale."

Reaching under the table, Merrick set his hand on Toby's thigh. "What about your family?"

Toby closed his eyes for a moment, another bitter breath escaping his lips at the multitude of painful explanations coming out today.

Merrick gave his leg a gentle squeeze. "You can tell me, Toby."

Refocusing on the young man, Toby sighed yet again. "No help there. Dad died when I was four, and my mother had a series of boyfriends."

"Wow. Was she supportive of you being gay?"

His mouth stretched in a sickly smile. "No, and the drunker the jerk she was dating got, the worse things were." Memories of the terrors of his teen years crowded to the fore of Toby's mind. His mother screaming into his face, the backhands across his cheek from her boyfriends. Too many nights, he'd huddled inside his room with the dresser against the door to shield himself from their abuse.

Merrick's hand slipped away from Toby's leg.

Toby steeled himself. He knew this part all too well. The sympathetic look, the noises of empathy—followed by the declaration that Toby was too damaged to date or even be around.

Merrick leaned his elbows on the table. His eyes reflected no sympathy, just a warm admiration. "You're incredible. You know that, right?" He shook his head, smiling a little, and lifted his sandwich to take another bite.

Cocking his head to the side, Toby furrowed his brow in confusion. His date wasn't following the familiar script. "Incredible? How do you figure that?"

Merrick finished his bite. "You should eat your sandwich." As Toby lifted the bread, Merrick continued. "You've been knocked way down. Instead of giving up or going back to an abusive situation, you picked yourself up, dusted off the adversity, and moved forward. You're angry—and, dammit, you should be—but you're still standing."

Merrick had stated a preference for men who had it all together. *Together* was the last thing he felt. "Things seem like they're collapsing around me." He brought the roast beef to his mouth and took a bite. The perfect combination of horseradish and pickle mixed with the beef, and he savored the comforting tastes.

"You're going to be just fine. This thing with Mark will pass, whether you stay at this job or find another. Just keep moving forward. Don't look back at his shit or the way he screwed you." Merrick raised an eyebrow. "Or did you screw him?"

Toby chuckled at the change of subject. "Um, he was on the bottom most of the time," he murmured.

"So, there you go." He did his best impression of an old Greek man complete with a little shrug and emphasizing his point with his hands – straight out of *My Big, Fat, Greek Wedding*.

Toby erupted in laughter. "I love that movie."

With another wink, Merrick lifted his glass. "Changing the subject… Where would you like to grab happy hour tonight?" He finished off the water.

"How about the pub in West Seattle? Or is there somewhere closer to your place you'd like to go?" Toby realized he didn't really know anything about Merrick's neighborhood. The other night, Merrick had refused his invitation for a ride home, and he rarely had reason to journey to the peninsula just across the bay from West Seattle. Merrick, though, gave him more than enough reason to make the circuitous route to the somewhat remote section of Seattle. "You said you're in Magnolia, right?"

Merrick beamed. "Yup. I frequent a nice pub over there. It's on McGraw, in that little business district."

"Text me the address, and I'll meet you there around six."

Pulling his cell from his pocket, Merrick typed out a quick message. "I need to head back, but I just sent you the address." He slipped his cell into his pocket and wrapped up the remainder of his sandwich.

"You've got it memorized?" Toby's phone dinged as he stood. He strode to the counter and grabbed two bags from the bussing station and returned. "Here, put your sandwich in this."

"Thanks. Yeah, it's close to the corner, and I know my address is only a couple of blocks away."

They bagged their sandwiches and headed out into the afternoon. A cool breeze blew along the street, and Toby shivered.

Merrick wrapped an arm around him. "It's a bit brisk out here. Don't worry about Mark. Everything's going to be great."

"Thanks." Though he didn't feel like it would be, he was glad of Merrick's optimism and willingness to listen. The best part—he didn't reject Toby and run.

Pulling him into an embrace, Merrick kissed his head again. "See you later."

Toby lingered in the embrace, not wanting it to end. Merrick also didn't pull away. With some reluctance and a final squeeze, Toby stepped back. "I'm looking forward to tonight."

"Me, too." Merrick wriggled his eyebrows.

As Merrick turned with a final wave and hurried up the street, Toby glanced across the roadway. Marsha stood watching him with Mark at her side. There were frowns on both their faces. Another swell of anger crashed over Toby. He turned his back on them and headed toward the parking garage.

CHAPTER SIX

Parking his Mini on McGraw at ten minutes before six, Toby checked his face in the mirror. He'd calmed considerably since his lunch with Merrick, even with the unwelcomed witnesses to their hug. Wrapped in Merrick's arms, nothing else seemed to matter but the warmth and safety his embrace engendered. Mark's poor attempts at comfort had never felt that good, seeming to sap away his energy rather than restoring his confidence.

He flipped the visor up, pushed open the door, and climbed out into the cool evening. Fortunately, the crisp breeze earlier in the day had subsided, but there was still a definite wet chill in the air. One of those special Seattle evenings that left one shivering, regardless of the heaviness of the coat or the stillness of the wind. He hugged his jacket closer and crossed the sidewalk to enter the pub Merrick had suggested.

A tall Asian woman with long, dark hair approached him. "Hi, there. Table for one?"

"Actually, I'm meeting someone." His eyes scanned the restaurant.

Her face lit up in a smile. "Oh, are you Merrick's friend?"

He swung his gaze back at her. "Uh, yeah."

"He's already here. Let me take you back." She led the way through the crowded pub. Not unlike his haunt in West Seattle, wooden tables dotted the room, and a row of booths lined the wall. She stopped at the last booth in a secluded corner.

Looking up from his phone, Merrick smiled warmly and scooted out to stand. "Glad you found it. Cindy, this is Toby."

The waitress grabbed his hand and shook it. "Nice to meet you. Merrick's been gushing about this great guy he met." She leaned into Merrick. "You're right. He's hot."

Toby laughed as Merrick's face reddened even in the dim light of the bar.

With a grin of her own, Cindy focused on Merrick. "Cider or wine tonight?"

Lifting an eyebrow, Merrick addressed Toby. "What's your pleasure?"

Toby shrugged. "Wine sounds good."

Before he could ask for the wine list, Merrick turned to Cindy. "Let's go with the bottle I asked about."

"Coming up." She bustled away.

Closing the gap between them, Merrick gave Toby a hug, lingering for a few moments instead of the quick bro-hug Toby would expect in an unfamiliar bar.

"Thanks for coming all the way over here." Merrick released him, letting a hand linger on his arm. "Can I take your jacket?"

A flush of pleasure and slight embarrassment spread across Toby's face. "Sure." He unzipped the coat and shrugged it off his shoulders.

Merrick held the collar as Toby pulled his arms from the sleeves. He hung it on a hook protruding from the side of the booth. "Have a seat."

Scooting onto the bench seat, Toby's eyes focused on a box on the table. Plain brown paper covered the outside, and a red, fabric ribbon was tied in a neat bow on the top. He lifted his gaze to Merrick's as his tall date slipped into the booth. "What's this?"

"It's for you." He bit his lower lip in an adorably uncertain way. "I hope you like it."

"Merrick, you didn't have to get me anything." Toby couldn't help the excitement that filled him at the thought of this handsome, sweet guy offering him a gift.

Merrick gave him a wink. "Wooing." He nodded to the box. "Open it."

Carefully untying the bow, Toby let the ribbon fall away and pulled off the two pieces of tape holding the paper together. The box beneath was from his favorite chocolatier in Seattle. Lifting the lid, four dark chocolate truffles nestled inside the box.

The familiar swirls and patterns on the tops of the truffles made him look up at Merrick. "How did you know?"

Again, the younger man tapped his nose and grinned. "Do you like them?"

"They're my favorite. Thank you." Where did Merrick get his information regarding Toby's favorites? All four dark chocolate—one coconut, one sea-salt, the third cashew butter, and the last huckleberry.

Cindy returned with the bottle Merrick ordered and two wine glasses. She showed Toby the label, and his eyes popped. A 2014 Portteus old-vine zinfandel. He nodded dumbly, and she proceeded to pop the cork before handing it to him. He sniffed the familiar scent of his favorite wine then set the cork on the table. She poured a small amount into his wine glass.

Swirling the smoky-red liquid, he brought the glass to his nose and inhaled the berry overtones of the tannins. He took a sip, and the rich flavors danced across his taste buds.

"Perfect." He turned to Merrick as she poured them both full glasses. "Your sources are amazing."

Merrick's smile spread from ear to ear.

After Cindy left them, Toby sat back in the booth, contentment settling in as the wine warmed him.

Merrick raised his glass. "To difficult days with happy endings."

With an arched eyebrow and a smirk, Toby touched his glass to Merrick's. "To wooing and mysterious sources."

They both sipped their wine. Merrick didn't take his gaze off of Toby, and the excitement and warmth of the connection kept Toby captivated.

Cindy returned with a large platter and two smaller plates.

Merrick piped up as she set the dishes on the table, "I ordered calamari. Hope that's okay for an appetizer."

Another favorite. "This isn't fair, you know."

His smile faded a little. "How do you mean?"

"You have this amazing source feeding you all my secrets, and I don't have any idea what kinds of things to do for you." With a start, he finally realized who Merrick's source was, and he chided himself for being slow on the uptake. *Stazi.* He'd have to remember to send her a little note later on.

"Not to worry." He wriggled his eyebrows. "I'm the one who's doing the wooing."

Cindy laughed. "There's tarter and a mustard aioli on the platter, and malt vinegar on the table. Is there anything else I can get you two?"

Turning to her, Toby shook his head. "No, unless you've got some secrets to dish on this handsome guy."

She leaned in conspiratorially. "Come by sometime when he's not here, and I'll give you the lowdown."

He glanced across the table at his date with a triumphant grin. "I just might do that."

She moved away to another table as Merrick unrolled his silverware and stuck his fork into one of the lemon slices. "Mind if I squeeze some lemon juice on these?"

"Not at all." Toby sat back as Merrick used the fork, and his thumb and middle finger, to spread the lemon juice over the lightly-breaded squid.

Dislodging the spent wedge, Merrick set the fork down on the table. "Dig in."

Toby scooped some of the calamari onto his plate. "Any more surprises for me this evening?"

Merrick shrugged. "Depends on how you play your cards."

With a chuckle, Toby dipped one piece of squid into

the aioli and took a bite. The calamari were perfect, not at all rubbery, with the flavor of the seasoning and breading complementing the seafood without a lot of extra spice. "I think you've discovered the right way to woo me. This is delicious." He took another bite.

"What's the old saying? The way to a man's heart…" Merrick took his own bite, swallowing and then sipping his wine. He placed the glass on the table. "What did you do this afternoon after I went back to work?"

Toby wrinkled his nose. "Honestly, I stewed a little about the whole Mark situation." That was putting it mildly, but he didn't want to go too far into how much he dreaded work tomorrow. "Tell me about your day. Anything interesting or fun?"

Merrick let his head fall to the right a little as his gaze lifted for a moment before resettling on Toby's. "Not really. There were the usual folks coming and going. A few upper management types that think they're better than everyone else, but otherwise most of the people I interact with are friendly."

"Do you like the concierge work?" Toby finished his glass, and then picked up the bottle and topped off Merrick's before refilling his own.

He shrugged, contemplating his wine. "It pays the bills. I'll probably stick with it for a while, but, eventually, I'd like to find something in my field."

Surprised, Toby's gaze locked on Merrick. "What's your degree in?"

Merrick grimaced. "That's the thing. I didn't finish. My grandfather died, and I dropped out of college to help my grandma." Merrick's face lost some of its light. "She passed away last fall, and I miss her a lot. They both were there for me when I came out to my family. Neither of them batted an eyelash, but my dad had a hard time accepting me."

"I'm sorry. All my grandparents are gone now." He thought about his mother's parents and how much he'd loved spending time at their farm as a kid. The calm in the storm of his childhood.

"My folks are great, now," Merrick continued. The smile Toby loved returned.

"Grandma let my dad have it after we lost Grandpa, and he apologized to me. You'll love my parents."

Toby paused for a moment. "I will?" When did he agree to meet Merrick's parents?

His date didn't miss a beat. "Yup. Want some dinner?"

Though he didn't want the evening with Merrick to end so soon, the calamari were enough for him. "I finished that sandwich at about two-thirty, so I'm pretty satisfied right now."

"Could I tempt you with some strawberry rhubarb pie, then?" Merrick chewed at his lip for a moment. "I have some back at my place. It's only a couple blocks away."

Toby wondered if there was more than pie waiting for him at Merrick's apartment. A flurry of nerves made his stomach do a little flip. Mark was the last person he'd been with, opting to satisfy himself without any further complications. Stazi's words from the past about not dating a coworker, advice he reminded himself he hadn't taken before, came back to haunt him. But Merrick wasn't a coworker. He worked in the same building, but if things didn't work out, there wouldn't be any discomfort coming into the office every day—not from Merrick, anyway.

And then there was the pie. Yet another of his favorites. His best friend had obviously fed Merrick with lots of ammunition to compliment his wooing arsenal.

Toby narrowed his eyes and smiled. "Yeah. I'd like to see your place." His hand shook a little as he reached for his glass.

Merrick seemed just as nervous, fidgeting with his napkin. "Great, I'll get the check." He signaled Cindy, held out his palm, and mimicked writing. She nodded and hurried to the bar.

The buzz from the wine helped with his courage. Though not anywhere near drunk, his memories of how Mark hurt him and his fear of dating anyone else seemed a little ridiculous. Kind, caring, and romantic, Merrick was nothing like his traitorous ex-boyfriend.

Cindy brought the bill. She dodged Toby's reach, and Merrick snagged it.

Toby furrowed his brow. "Hey, you said I could get happy hour."

Producing his credit card, Merrick quickly handed it and the bill to Cindy. "True, but this isn't happy hour."

Toby grabbed his phone from his pocket, lit up the display, and turned it to show Merrick the time. "See, you ordered well within the hours of happiness."

Merrick laughed. "This is a *wooing* happy hour."

After Cindy walked away, Toby frowned, but warmth still poured through him. "Merrick."

"You've had a rough day," he soothed, his voice full of warmth and reason. "I'm the one who ordered the bottle of wine. You can get the next one. Promise." White teeth flashed in a disarming grin.

With a sigh of defeat, Toby's lips parted in a small smile. "Thank you." His pride was a little damaged, but Merrick's attentions and kindness made him feel special for the first time in a long time. Come to think of it, no guy had ever paid this much attention to him, or went to this much trouble.

Cindy returned, handing the slip and card to Merrick. "You gents have a great night." She winked at Toby. "I'm here on Monday if you want some ideas."

Merrick arched an eyebrow. "Hmm. That might be the end of your tip."

Laughing, Toby caught Merrick's worried glance at the waitress. "Don't worry, I'll make up for any shortfall."

She giggled as she left their table.

Merrick glanced from her retreating form to Toby. A dark brow curved, and he drummed his fingers on the table. "This may have been a miscalculation."

"You can't have the only advantage." Toby stood, his stomach fluttering. He grabbed his jacket from the hook and slipped it on, and then snagged the box of chocolates from the table, placing them in his pocket. "Ready?"

With a nod, Merrick quickly signed the slip, and Toby noticed he'd left a generous tip for Cindy. Another good sign. Mark had been terrible about leaving a decent tip, even when the service was exceptional. Toby had gotten used to looking at the bill and would usually hang back to leave the server extra cash.

He wasn't pleased to see how much the wine and calamari had cost the concierge. "Merrick, please let me help with this."

With a shake of his head and a firm stare, Merrick rose. "No way." He took Toby's hand. "I want to do this for you. Come on. My place isn't far." He stuck the cork in the half-full bottle of wine and slipped it into his courier bag. They made their way along the row of booths and out into the night.

The moment their fingers intertwined, a jolt of electricity surged through Toby's body. Much stronger than when they'd first shaken hands. The attraction and energy coursing through their connection deepened with each step through the cold evening.

When they reached the apartment building, Merrick let go and dug in his bag for the keys. Opening the door with a nervous smile, he stood back to allow Toby to enter, then followed him in and made sure the glass doors framed in metal were closed.

"I'm on the third floor." Merrick led him down a corridor with white walls and the occasional framed floral picture to a plain door. Though neat and tidy, the building was a little older, likely a nineteen-eighties construction. "I usually take the stairs. Is that okay with you?"

"Sure." With a little tremble, Toby fought to get his nerves under control.

Raising an eyebrow in concern, Merrick took one of his shaking hands. "Doing okay?"

"Honestly, I'm pretty nervous right now." Toby stared

at the floor.

Merrick raised Toby's hand and brushed his lips over the palm. "Don't be."

A shiver of pleasure made Toby close his eyes for a moment. When they opened again, Merrick had taken a step closer. Toby gasped as Merrick released his hand and wrapped his arm around Toby's waist.

Toby lay his head on Merrick's lean chest, listening to the rapidly beating heart inside and inhaling the clean scent of his body. He held onto the young man, his eyes closed, and basked in his warmth.

Merrick kissed his head like he'd done just after lunch. "The pie was an excuse to get you to come home with me. I mean, I do have some pie, and we can have some…uh, if you want."

The nervous chatter made Toby chuckle. "I'm a little scared, Merrick." He stayed in the tight embrace but lifted his head to gaze into Merrick's eyes. "Every minute with you shows me I don't have to be afraid of a relationship, but I'm still terrified of ending up with a broken heart again."

Merrick held him, leaning down and brushing their lips together. "I'd never intentionally hurt you, Toby. Never." He sealed the promise with a firm kiss.

Sliding his eyelids shut again, Toby lost himself in the perfection of the kiss, and the explosions of warmth and pleasure pushed away some of his trepidation. Merrick's tongue traced Toby's lips, until they yielded and he gained entry. Toby's hands were all over Merrick's body, taking in every inch he could reach of his date's lean but strong frame.

After a few moments, Merrick broke the kiss and stepped back. His gaze glittered in the stairwell light. "May I take you upstairs?" he asked breathily. His hands sought Toby's.

Toby could only nod, his mind blown away by the rush of overwhelming feelings and emotions, and his body ached for another embrace. He allowed himself to be pulled along behind Merrick, who led him up two flights of steps. Once in the hallway, they hurried to his apartment door.

Merrick released one of Toby's hands while he fumbled in his bag for his keys again, but kept a firm grip on Toby's other hand.

Producing the key, he unlocked the door, pushed it open, and dragged Toby inside. He pushed the strap over his head and dropped his courier bag onto the floor.

Not bothering to take in his surroundings, Toby rushed into Merrick's waiting arms as the door slammed shut. Their lips met again, and Toby found his back pressed against a wall as Merrick's hands roamed freely across his body, tugging at zippers and pulling at buttons.

Wanting to feel Merrick's bare body gliding against his own, Toby pulled Merrick's shirttails from his slacks and slid his hands up the hairy skin of Merrick's flat stomach. Their lips pressed against each other's harder, and the kiss quickly intensified.

Merrick moved his mouth down from Toby's chin, nibbling and sucking at his neck. Jolts of pleasure held Toby in place and ripped a moan from his throat, while

Merrick's nimble fingers pried apart the remaining buttons and nearly ripped open his dress shirt.

"You're beautiful, Toby," Merrick whispered. "I want you so bad." He kissed his way across Toby's chest and clamped his lips around an erect nipple.

Fire burned across Toby's skin as Merrick nibbled and tongued the sensitive nub. Pressure built in his slacks, and his erection strained against the fabric and zipper.

Paralyzed with pleasure, he let out a whimper and squirmed against the wall, abandoning all hope of his fingers working to free Merrick from his clothes. Merrick gave the nipple one last swipe of his tongue and continued down the line of sandy hair leading from his chest to his waist.

Having already undone the belt holding up Toby's slacks during their initial kiss, Merrick knelt and pushed the leather out of the way. He unclasped the metal hook holding the pants closed. Forcing the zipper open, he let the slacks fall to the floor, sliding his fingers under the elastic of Toby's briefs.

Now freed of its confines, Toby's cock jutted straight out from his groin. Merrick slid his fingers lightly over the shaft, making Toby's head bump back against the wall from the sensation. His eyes closed while his body shuddered and another moan escaped his lips.

Merrick's husky voice broke through his haze of sensations. "Toby?"

Prying his lids open, he focused on Merrick, inches away from the head of his cock and staring up at him. "Yes?"

"Anything I should be concerned about?" Merrick slowly slid his tongue along the underside of the shaft.

In a strangled tone, Toby croaked, "No." Another moan. "No one since Mark."

Merrick gently sucked each ball into his mouth.

Toby's hands slapped against the wall as another jolt of pleasure made his knees shake. "Tests all good." His eyes rolled as Merrick ran his tongue from balls to head and sucked in the first couple inches of his shaft. Toby nearly shook apart under the expert pleasuring of his dick.

Merrick came up for air, letting the head pass his lips with a pop. "Want some pie?"

"What?" Toby's eyes flew open as he swung his attention down to Merrick. It took a moment to register the mischievous twinkle in his date's eyes and the little smirk edging across his lips.

Standing, Merrick took his hand. "Step out of your slacks, and let's go to the bedroom."

Toby kicked off his shoes and pushed off the pants legs, leaving his trousers in a tangle on the floor. His briefs stretched across his thighs, but were high enough not to impede his walking.

They crossed the threshold into Merrick's tiny bedroom. A double bed, extended at the end, consumed all the space in the room, except for a narrow walkway along the side to allow access to the closet.

"Sorry it's so tight in here." He sat on the mattress and looked up at Toby, his hands fisting on his thighs. "I want you so bad right now, but are you ready for this? Once I have you naked and in bed with me, I won't want to let you go until we have to leave for work tomorrow." Merrick's gaze held a combination of pleading and hunger.

Toby marveled at the man before him. No one had ever wanted him like this. Certainly not Mark, even when they'd first gotten together. Meeting Merrick's gaze full on, Toby conceded he wanted this man just as much. His body nearly cramping with need, Toby's cock lengthened, stretching over the waistband of his briefs. After pushing his underwear to the floor and dropping his jacket and shirt from his shoulders, Toby held out his hand. "Stand up."

Merrick grasped his hand and stood. His chest rose and fell with deeply gusting breaths. "Does this mean you're staying here tonight?"

"Damned right, and you're overdressed." A confidence he hadn't felt in years surged inside of Toby.

With his mouth curving to an easy smile, Merrick's hand pressed gently against Toby's face, and his thumbs caressed along his cheeks. "You're such a beautiful guy."

His eyes were mesmerizing, holding Toby's gaze in their dazzling pools of blue until he moved forward and pressed his lips against Toby's mouth.

The frantic entry into the apartment gave way to something slower and achingly tender. As the kiss lingered, Merrick's hands glided along Toby's skin, sending shockwaves of pleasure crashing from head to toe. With his palms settling on Toby's ass, Merrick pulled their bodies together.

Toby wove his arms up Merrick's back and settled his hands on the slender shoulders. Pulling away from the kiss but still holding on, Toby again gazed into the sapphire that made his heart skip a beat. "Let's get your clothes off. I want to feel all of you."

With a ghost of a smile and a brief chuckle, Merrick kissed his nose. "I guess that means I'm yours."

Slowly unbuttoning Merrick's shirt, he ran his hand over the tufts of hair on his partner's chest. He pushed the shirt from Merrick's shoulders then sank to his knees. Toby's mouth salivated as the massive bulge in Merrick's crotch pushed against the restraining fabric. With trembling hands, Toby pulled away the belt, unhooked the pants, and lowered the zipper. The large cock throbbed, outlined by the tented briefs. Toby licked the covered shaft and wrapped his mouth around the head.

Gasping, Merrick placed a large hand on Toby's shoulder. "Wow, that feels good." His voice came out breathy and low.

Toby pulled back and hooked his fingers under the waistband of the straining underwear. "Just you wait." He tugged downward and dove onto the freed head.

The hand on his shoulder tightened, and Merrick let out a long groan. "Oh, Toby." His legs shook, and Toby followed him as he lowered himself onto the bed.

Mark had been quiet and detached during sex, choosing to lay on his back and let Toby either ride him or suck him without much reciprocation. Merrick murmured encouragements, running fingers through Toby's wavy locks and clearly enjoying everything Toby's tongue was doing to his shaft.

"I'm getting close already," Merrick wheezed, pushing

himself up to sit and gently pressing against Toby's shoulder. "Let me suck you."

Toby glanced up at the absolute longing in Merrick's voice. He gave the head a lick and released it from his mouth. "Really?"

With pupil's blown, Merrick breathed heavily. "Please, Toby. I want to taste you again so badly."

Complying with Merrick's request, Toby rose. He raked his gaze over the lean man on the bed and, before Merrick could take Toby into his mouth, climbed onto the bed and lay with his head next to Merrick's thigh. "Let's suck each other."

Hunger burned in Merrick's eyes as he leaned back and drew Toby's dick into his warm mouth, tightening his lips around the shaft and applying an amazing suction.

Toby's eyes rolled back, and he savored the eruption of pleasure spreading over his body. At least three years had gone by since anyone had sucked him, and, judging by the growing tingles and heat in his balls, he wouldn't last long.

Forcing his eyes open, he concentrated on returning the incredible sensations Merrick gave him. He polished the large, mushroom head then slipped his lips down the throbbing shaft.

Merrick's moans vibrated around his own cock, and the tingling grew as his balls tightened in their sack. Rapidly approaching the point of no return, Toby tried to pull back, but Merrick clamped a hand on his thigh and pulled him deeper. The choking around his cock made his legs tremble then straighten tightly, and he shouted out his release, spilling into Merrick's throat.

Pulling off Toby's dick, Merrick's legs also tightened, and he roared as spurt after spurt shot into Toby's mouth. Swallowing quickly, Toby concentrated on catching everything his lover had to offer. Tremors shook Merrick's body as he turned onto his back, dislodging his cock from Toby's mouth.

Weakly, Toby dragged himself around and lay his head onto Merrick's chest. The wiry hairs tickled his cheek. Merrick's arm snaked around his shoulders and pulled him tighter against his body.

"Thank you," he breathed heavily, kissing Toby's forehead.

Heat burned at Toby's cheeks. "Sorry I came so fast. It's been a long time." He kept his head on Merrick's pec, listening to the slowing beat of the man's heart and finding it difficult to keep his eyes open.

"Don't apologize for something so special." Merrick softly chuckled. "I shot like a teenager."

Toby snuggled closer. "I could fall asleep just like this."

"Let's get some rest then." With a groan, Merrick gently dislodged Toby's head from his chest and pushed himself off the bed. He tugged the comforter out from under Toby and pulled it back. Climbing back onto the bed, he pulled the covers over the top of them and lay on his back. Toby reclaimed his spot on Merrick's chest, and sleep quickly washed over him.

CHAPTER SEVEN

T HE ALARM ON his cell went off, filling the room with *Manic Monday* by the Bangles. Toby groaned as sleep continued to tug at his body, trying to lure him back into its comfortable embrace.

As his mind screamed at him to wake up, he realized he wasn't on the small futon he called a bed in his apartment. He also quickly became aware of an arm draped over his chest. Sucking in a startled breath, Toby struggled to figure out where he was, but quickly remembered falling asleep in Merrick's arms. With a comfortable sigh, he turned onto his side to face the lazily smiling man.

"Good morning." A groggy Merrick leaned into him and gave him a peck on his cheek, tightening his embrace. "Did you sleep well?"

The memory of the night before came flooding back as he continued his roll onto his side and stared at the man next to him. "After that amazing blowjob, yeah," he said, his voice a little rusty.

Closing his eyes again, Merrick patted Toby's side. "What time is it?"

A frown tugged at Toby's mouth as his head cleared of sleep and began working out the math for the commute, assuming his phone's alarm had gone off at the right time. "A little after six. I've got to be downtown by seven-thirty. What time do you go in?"

Merrick sighed and blinked open his eyes. "Seven. I had hoped to make you breakfast, but if we don't get out of Magnolia in about half an hour, we're stuck on the bridge for a long time." He smirked. "Though I'd be happy to be stuck with you, Mister Eighties."

Laughing at the song lyric, Toby grabbed his phone before the second alarm went off. He turned off the alarm clock feature while he glanced at Merrick sitting up and stretching his long arms.

A dusting of dark hair spread between the quarter-sized nipples on Merrick's sinewy chest. His arms settled onto the comforter, and he gave Toby a lopsided grin with sleepy eyes and fly-away hair.

Toby set the phone onto the floor and pounced on Merrick. "I wish we had time to do lots of things this morning." He kissed the surprised man hard and pushed him back onto the pillow. "We only sucked each other off last night, and I want to explore every inch of you."

With a goofy grin, Merrick trailed a finger over Toby's shoulder, sending cascades of tingles down his back. "You got every inch last night."

"Not true. There's six feet and six inches of you still to explore." Toby kissed his neck, savoring the slightly salty taste.

Laughing, Merrick rolled their bodies over until Toby was on his back. "We'd get fired."

"At this exact moment, I wouldn't care." He struggled

under Merrick, trying to get at the prize still wrapped in the sheets swirling around his waist.

"You'd care once we got out of bed." Merrick nodded toward the bedroom door. "Come on, sexy man. Let's get a shower." Merrick pushed himself off of Toby and let the sheet fall away to reveal his body as his feet touched the floor. He flicked on a small light set into the wall.

Toby whistled. "I didn't get a good look at you last night. Wow." His gaze traveled up Merrick's long, hairy legs and settled on the tree-trunk growing from his neatly trimmed crotch. Toby's cock, already half-hard with his usual morning stiffness, pulsed.

Turning a deep shade of red, Merrick turned away. "You're a charmer."

After clambering out of bed, Toby stood behind Merrick and admired the firm butt and slender, muscled back. "Nah, I just appreciate beauty in all its forms." He pressed his now fully erect cock between Merrick's legs. "And your form is definitely beautiful."

With an arched eyebrow, Merrick turned to consider him, amusement and indecision dancing in his eyes. "You're just trying to lure me back to bed."

"Is it working?" He kissed along the soft skin and ran his hands from Merrick's shoulders to his waist.

With a ragged breath, Merrick shook his head. "No."

Toby lowered his voice and wrapped his arms around Merrick's body, letting his fingers tickle the low-hanging balls under a fully hard cock. "Are you sure?"

Stepping forward, Merrick sighed heavily. "Let's take a shower." He spun around, facing Toby and wrapping him in an embrace that had their cocks pressed together. "Come back tonight, and I promise we'll make up for what we're missing this morning."

With a final kiss, Toby gave Merrick a squeeze. "I'll hold you to it."

TOBY DROPPED MERRICK off at the front of their building at three minutes to seven, then pulled around the block and found a spot in the parking garage.

Instead of taking the stairs up to the lobby, he exited the garage and walked down the hill to his favorite coffee shop. He didn't have to be at work for another half hour and could use a little caffeine pick-me-up.

"Hey, Toby. Your usual Americano?" LaToya, the feisty barista he'd come to adore, shot him a grin.

"Sounds good. I'm dragging a bit today." With the short but pleasurable night, he'd need all the help he could get to make it through the day.

"But you have such a glow about you this morning," she cooed. "If I didn't know better, I'd say you met someone." Pulling the lever to grind some beans, she winked at him.

"As a matter of fact…" His words trailed off as Mark stepped into the coffee shop. His back and shoulders stiffened. Another confrontation with Mark was the last thing he wanted, especially after such a magical evening.

"Well, congratulations." The espresso machine whirred as she rang him up. "Anything else?"

"Yeah. Two of your breakfast croissants and add a cup

of drip for Merrick." From the corner of his eye, he caught Mark's wave to get his attention, but quickly turned back to LaToya.

She gave him a sly smile. "Aw, you're taking your guy some breakfast." She took his credit card, ran it, then turned back to the espresso machine. "It'll be up in just a minute."

He moved to the side to let the next customer order, hoping Mark would let him be. No such luck.

"Hey." Mark sidled up to him. "I didn't see you after lunch."

Keeping his tone even, Toby watched LaToya work. "Roger gave me half a day off."

"Oh. Why?"

Toby spun to face him, his brow furrowing as he fought to keep his temper in check. "Maybe it's because the Ghost of Assholes Past is now working in the office right next to mine at the only job I've been able to land in over two years."

Lifting his hands in front of him, Mark took a step back. "Geez, Toby. Chill."

A throat cleared behind him, and both of them turned to see LaToya narrowing her eyes at Mark.

"Is there a problem?" Her head did an attitude bob, hands planted on her hips.

Toby was glad he wasn't the focus of her disdain.

"No problem, ma'am. Uh, see you at work, Toby." Mark moved away and stepped to the end of the line.

Toby turned to face her. "Remind me never to piss you off."

She pushed the two drinks and the sandwiches across the countertop. "Honey, I doubt you could ever do that."

Fishing in his pocket, he pulled out his wallet and threw a five-dollar bill into the tip jar. "Have a great day, LaToya."

"Back at ya, Toby." She turned to the next customer in line as Toby moved to the bussing station.

After grabbing a couple napkins, he headed for the door. With a quick glance at the line, he saw Mark frowning as he tried to chat with LaToya and realized that his smooth lines didn't pass her bullshit detector.

Dumb ass. He chuckled, pushed open the shop door, and stepped into the cool morning. The light changed at Fourth and Seneca just as he got there, and he waited at the corner.

"Toby, hold up."

He glanced back to see Mark hurrying up the street with a cup in his hand. *Shit.* He didn't have much of a choice. There was absolutely no reason to cross to the other side of Fourth, and he'd likely be late for work or not be able to stop to see Merrick if he went back down to Third and orbited the building.

Mark caught up to him and offered a tentative smile. "Thanks. Can we talk?"

With a heavy sigh, Toby stepped back from the corner and stood with his shoulder leaning against the wall of a stone building. Best to get this over with. "You have five minutes."

"You look well." His gaze dropped, and he shuffled his feet.

"Thanks." Toby was careful to keep his tone neutral. He didn't want Mark to take his willingness to listen as a sign of encouragement. He just wanted this to be over before he exploded at Mark and threw his and Merrick's coffee into his treasonous ex's face.

"I went by the house last night, but I didn't see your Mini there."

Fighting back his anger, Toby's words came out clipped and frosty. "There are two reasons for that. One, I *wasn't* home last night, but the second and more pertinent reason why my Mini wasn't there is that I don't own that house anymore."

Mark looked down. "Oh. You sold it?"

Toby's face burned so hot he wouldn't have been surprised if smoke rose from his ears. "No, Mark. I *lost* the house because no one in this town would hire me. When you suddenly lose both your job and your live-in boyfriend, it's impossible to make a mortgage payment."

With eyes wide, Mark looked up. "Shit. I'm sorry, Toby."

"Not sorry enough." Toby narrowed his own gaze. "Much as I enjoyed this painful trip down memory lane, I need to get my friend his breakfast, and then get upstairs to the office. Unfortunately, I'll have to see you there."

The light changed, and he pushed off the wall, leaving Mark open-mouthed and staring. He made sure no idiot was barreling down the street as he stepped into the crosswalk. His mood only half an hour ago had been bright, and he'd felt like he could take on the entire world. The interaction with Mark had soured his morning considerably.

Merrick noticed immediately as Toby pushed the revolving door and stepped into the lobby. He hopped off his chair and hurried across the shiny floor. "Are you okay?" His face screwed up in concern, Merrick laid his hand on Toby's shoulder.

"Yeah." He handed Merrick the drip coffee and one of the sandwiches, struggling to brighten his attitude. "I brought you breakfast, since I nearly made us late this morning."

A smirk tugged the sides of Merrick's mouth up. "You dropped that soap on purpose."

Immediately feeling better just being in Merrick's presence, he chuckled. "Guilty."

Merrick gave his cheek a kiss. "You're awesome."

From the corner of his eye, Toby saw Mark push through the revolving door in time to see the kiss. With a petulant frown on his lips, his ex scowled and glared at Merrick before storming across the lobby toward the elevator bank.

Looking between the two men, Toby grumbled. "I was doing so well until I had to interact with that asshole at the coffee shop."

Merrick kept his hand firmly planted on Toby's shoulder as he glanced at the still frowning man.

Toby's eyes widened as Merrick steered him closer and planted a full kiss on his lips. Much as he'd have loved to drop their breakfast and ravage Merrick, he knew this PDA wasn't the best idea. Still, he enjoyed the feel of Merrick's lips molded on his own for a few moments before breaking away. Plus, he took some satisfaction Mark had to witness it.

With a glance back at the elevator bank, Toby was relieved to see Mark had gone. He turned back to Merrick. "I'm sorry I don't have time to eat breakfast with you, but I need to get upstairs."

"It's okay. Thank you so much for bringing me some coffee. The sandwich smells wonderful." He led Toby over to his podium and hopped up onto the stool. "Lunch plans?"

"I'm meeting Stazi at the little teriyaki place on Cherry. She probably wouldn't mind if you tagged along."

He shook his head. "You two probably need to chat about this whole Mark thing."

Toby nodded. "Thanks for understanding. I'm all yours after work, though." He faltered a moment. "That is, if you still want to spend the evening together."

Merrick's grin spread across his face. "I packed an extra set of clothes and my toothbrush in my backpack this morning—just in case you wanted to invite me back to your place."

Warmth filled Toby as his mood lightened, and genuine excitement for the evening filled him. "I'll take that as a yes. My bed isn't as comfortable as yours, but you're welcome to share it with me."

"I'm sure if I snuggle up next to you, I'll be just fine." Merrick gave him a quick peck on his lips. "Until tonight."

Roger stepped up to the podium. "Morning, Toby. Merrick. How are you guys doing?" He eyed Toby's clothes, but didn't say anything.

Toby felt heat rise up the back of his neck, knowing the fact he wore the same clothes as yesterday led Roger to an accurate conclusion regarding his and Merrick's activities the prior evening.

"We're doing great. How about you?" Merrick beamed.

The corners of Roger's mouth twitched. "Not as great as you two obviously are, but it's been a good morning so far. Ready for a busy day, Toby?"

He nodded, though he wasn't sure he was ready to face a day with Mark nearby. Or judging by his supervisor's grin, discussing his personal life. Although, perhaps Roger would have some ideas how Toby could do a little wooing of his own.

"Okay, drop by my office when you get upstairs." Roger headed for the elevator bay.

Toby met Merrick's amused glance and shrugged. "Gotta go."

"Have a good day, and I'll see you tonight." Merrick dug into the sandwich bag. "Bacon, egg, and cheese croissant? You're the best."

"See you tonight." Toby hurried to the elevator and jumped on the car Roger was in just as the doors started to close.

The shit-eating grin on his supervisor's face said all Toby needed to know about the topic of their meeting.

"So, Toby," Roger said, trying to sound casual. And failing. "Did you enjoy the afternoon away from the office?" His grin didn't falter in the slightest.

"It was needed, thank you." Toby kept his tone neutral.

The elevator stopped at floor twenty, and Toby and Roger stepped into the hallway. They strode into the reception area and signed in. Elsibeth waved at them and pointed to her headset.

"Come to my office, and we'll chat before you get started." Roger headed down the hall.

Pausing to glance at the board, Toby saw Mark was signed in, but Marsha was not. *Thank the heavens for small mercies.* He hurried after Roger, keeping his head down and focusing on getting to Roger's office without a run-in with the ex.

He turned the corner and stopped outside Roger's door, knocking on the frame.

Roger already had his coat off and was seated at his desk. "Come on in, and close the door."

Once inside, Toby sat at one of the chairs across from his supervisor and waited.

"Much as I want to dive in and discuss your personal life with sweet, young Merrick, we have to deal with another issue first." The smile was still there, but it was more of a kind, pitying smile than the big grin he'd received in the elevator.

Toby's stomach tightened, realizing Roger had asked him to close the door. "Okay, that sounds ominous." He could guess where this was going, and he considered just quitting before Roger had to fire him.

"I want you to know first and foremost, neither Herrington nor I want to lose you. However, Marsha has made some accusations I need answers to." Roger leaned forward, his elbows on his desk. "I need to know specifics on what happened at your last job that led to you quitting."

Toby sighed. So much for his improved mood. "I was accused of transferring company funds in some sort of money laundering scheme. Someone got my login and password to the bank when I was out of the office and wired the money."

Frowning, Roger's gaze was assessing and pointed. "What about a fob or some sort of security protocol?"

"The fob went missing, and I can only assume it was stolen." His shoulder sagged. "Mark knew I didn't do it, but he didn't vouch for me. I don't really understand why. That's why I freaked out yesterday when I saw him."

Roger paused, his stare giving nothing away. "But they didn't fire you or apparently level charges."

Toby shook his head. "Since they were able to retrieve the money, and because the fob was missing, they gave me the option to resign. None of us wanted a lawsuit, and I'd outperformed all of my predecessors in the job." He took a deep breath and exhaled. "That's when life got really hard."

"How so?"

"I couldn't get another job, which meant I couldn't make my mortgage payment, and I lost my house." Toby straightened his back and fixed his gaze on Roger. "This job is my last chance in Seattle. I honestly don't know what will happen if I have to leave town, and without this job, that's what I'll have to do." He inwardly cringed at the way that sounded. The last thing he wanted was to beg for his job, but his mind focused on Merrick, and he didn't want to leave just as he'd finally found someone special.

After considering for a moment, Roger sat back and nodded. "I believe you. From what I've already seen of Mark Spencer, I can tell he's a piece of work."

Toby sagged back in the chair, relief washing over him. "What about Herrington? Do you think he'll believe me?"

"I'll have a word with him. We're both extremely pleased with what you've done for us so far, and we like you personally quite a lot." He also sat back in his chair. "Herrington had a hard time buying the story Marsha was trying to peddle."

Toby blew out a breath that billowed his cheeks. "Thank you."

The grin returned, and Roger steepled his fingers together while his elbows perched on the armrests of his office chair. "Now that we're done with the unpleasant stuff, tell me all about you and Merrick."

TOBY CHECKED HIS phone as he hurried into the teriyaki restaurant. Stazi stood just inside, her arms crossed and her foot tapping. "Late." She threw her arms around him. "But I'm glad to see you."

He hugged her back. "How generous of you," he drawled.

"I buzzed you last night, but no one answered." She arched an eyebrow. "Booty call?"

He couldn't hide the grin forcing its way along his lips as he thought of the date and overnight with Merrick. "You're terrible."

She considered his face for a few moments as he tried to stare only at the menu on the wall. With an intake of air and bringing a hand to her mouth, she did a little happy dance right there in the middle of the restaurant.

The guy behind the counter shook his head, and his lips turned downward as he stared at her. "You ready to order?"

Toby stepped forward. "I have no idea who the crazy lady is." He grunted when Stazi elbowed him. "Can I get the chicken and gyoza platter?"

"One chicken gyoza. Anything else?" He wrote on his pad.

Toby fought a grin. "I'll get the crazy lady's food." After glancing back at her scowl, he leaned forward and loudly whispered, "It's nice to be charitable to the mentally insane."

Slapping his shoulder, she pushed her way to the counter. "Brat. Tofu teriyaki with extra salad."

Toby handed the guy his credit card and signed the slip.

"Five minutes, okay?" The guy didn't wait for their answer, simply turning and retreating into the kitchen.

The shop was on the sticky side of clean, but Toby loved coming here. This place was the sort of comfort-food restaurant he needed when the world felt like it was collapsing in on him. He and Stazi took the last empty table by the window.

She propped her elbows on the table and rested her chin in her hands. "Spill."

Toby knew she was already suspicious, but he didn't want to be that easy. "What makes you think I have anything to talk about?"

Her mouth twitched to the side. "You only ask me out for teriyaki when the shit hits the fan. Besides, I'm thinking last night was more than a booty call, but you definitely got some."

He laughed. "Okay, okay. You win."

She tapped her chin. "I think you went home with that delicious Merrick." She leaned closer. "Did you?"

He hesitated, pretending to consider whether to tell her anything.

Rolling her eyes, she made a show of checking her watch. "I have to be back to work in forty-five minutes."

"I went home with Merrick last night," he blurted. "He offered me pie, so how could I refuse?"

She leaned even closer, and her eyes narrowed. "How was the pie?"

Toby cleared his throat. "We never got to it, but we'll try again tonight."

Clapping her hands, she bounced in her chair. "Aw, honey. You finally ended your dry spell!" She pinched his cheek. "I'm so proud of you," she said, speaking in a voice she might use with a small child.

He pushed her hand away. "Knock that off. I'm glad you're happy about Merrick, but we have bigger things to discuss."

She sat back and eyed him. "I can only assume you

mean the asshole."

"Yeah. Mark." He launched into a description of their interaction at the coffee shop and the street corner earlier that morning.

She listened intently, all fun and teasing set aside. He loved that about her. She played with him a lot, but when the chips were down, she listened and offered unfiltered advice.

Their food arrived as he finished his story. After the waiter departed, Stazi broke apart her chopsticks and rubbed them together while staring thoughtfully out the window. "What I don't quite get is why Mark suddenly, after two years of silence, takes a job with you in the same office and relentlessly wants to talk to you." She expertly captured a square of tofu in her chopsticks and popped it into her mouth.

"I don't *care* why he wants to talk to me," Toby fumed. "He betrayed me and left me high and dry. I could have kept the house if he'd at least stuck by me." He pushed a gyoza around the plate, not all that interested in eating.

She laid her chopsticks on her plate and fixed him with her gaze. "Sweetie, why isn't he still working at Teller?"

"Uh…" He hadn't even considered why Mark had changed jobs.

"I know you don't have any contact with those people after what they did to you, but is there any way you could find out?"

Shaking his head, he turned and stared out the window. "I don't want anything to do with them. I doubt anyone there would even take my call, much less tell me anything." Even his two buddies in HR really couldn't talk to him, especially about Mark's employment or lack thereof.

"You said that Mark's position is temporary, right?" She took another bite of her lunch.

"Yeah." He glumly munched on a gyoza, sure Marsha would find a way to make him permanent if she could.

"Then wait him out," she said, snagging another piece of tofu. "He'll only be there a few months. I don't remember him being all that successful at Teller, and I'll bet he got fired or laid off. He'll fuck up this job as well." She popped the cube into her mouth.

"Maybe." He considered what she'd said. Perhaps the whole purpose of Mark being there was Marsha's way to get Toby out. She was clearly gunning for him. If Mark didn't accomplish her goal, she'd find another way. Although what she had against him in the first place mystified him.

"The other alternative is to look for something else." She quickly leaned forward as a piece of tofu slipped from her chopsticks and bounced off her chin. The escapee plopped back onto the bed of rice on her plate. "Shit."

He chuckled and passed her a napkin from the dispenser on the table. "It took me two years to find this job. I can't leave it."

"Nothing is worth being miserable. Not a job or a relationship." She dabbed the sauce off of her chin. "Try focusing on Merrick. Spend lots of nights together and develop your obvious feelings for him. He's a great guy from what I can tell."

Toby's face flushed with warmth. "Yeah, he is."

She balled up the napkin and tossed it at him, bouncing it off his nose. "And don't you even try to tell me you haven't fallen hard."

CHAPTER EIGHT

HERRINGTON'S VOICE BOOMED through the closed conference room door as Toby entered the reception area after returning to the office from his lunch with Stazi.

Though slightly muffled, Herrington must have been yelling, because Toby heard each word clearly. "If we lose Tobias, we'll lose Roger. If Roger Matthews goes, so help me I'll terminate this partnership. Unless you have proof, Marsha Fisher, you *will* back off of my employees!"

The warmth drained from Toby's cheeks as he glanced at Elsibeth. She shrugged and turned back to her computer.

Marsha's gravelly voice sounded just as loud through the wall. "I'll get proof. He's guilty as sin and should be in prison!"

Not to be left out, Angelica's shrill yell overpowered both of their voices. "*Enough!* The whole damned office can hear us."

The door to the conference room flew open, and Marsha stormed out, stopping short as she glared at Toby. Her face turned bright red.

Herrington thundered out the doorway and snarled at

her. "I'm warning you…"

Throwing up a hand in his face, she spun on her heel and stalked to her office, slamming the door after she stormed inside.

Angelica stood next to Herrington. Both of them stared at Toby until Angelica shook her head. "I'm sorry, Toby. I don't know what's gotten into her."

Frowning, Toby addressed his boss. "Do you want me to leave?"

Herrington stabbed a finger at him, fury blooming on his face. "Don't you dare. You are a valuable member of my team," he said, balling his fist. "I'll be damned if that harpy is going to run you out of here." He marched down the hall and around the corner.

Angelica joined Toby in the reception area. "Roger told us what you said this morning."

He stared at his shoes. "I guess he had to." Shame ripped at his entire being. Mark was no longer the one he had to worry about.

"She can't fire you, so don't let it trouble you. We'll sort this out." She smiled. "Did you have a good lunch?"

He barked a mirthless laugh. "Just dandy."

Patting his shoulder, she frowned. "It's not usually this bad here. Why don't you go to your office and try to relax for a bit before getting back to work?"

He nodded. "Thanks." Leaving the reception area, he trudged to the far side of the building and entered the office Roger had snagged for him yesterday. He sat heavily behind his desk and buried his head in his hands. "Shit, shit, shit."

His cell dinged, and he pulled himself together enough to read the incoming text. It was from Merrick.

Hope your day got better. Mine sucks. I'll meet you in West Seattle.

He unlocked the phone and typed a message back.

I can give you a ride after work.

The reply arrived quickly. *Already heading back to Magnolia. Lost my job today. Someone complained. Tell you about it tonight.*

He squeezed his eyes shut and hit his fist against the desk. Could this day get any worse?

He typed out another message. *Complained about what?*

The long pause in the reply made Toby nervous. After a couple minutes of staring at the phone, a text finally appeared.

Kissing.

The phone shook in his hand as the full implication of the single word hit him. He'd been responsible for getting Merrick fired. How could someone complain? It wasn't that big of a deal.

His mind flashed back to the moment they'd kissed. Mark had stalked past with a glare firmly leveled at Merrick.

A haze of red swirled over Toby's vision, his rage bubbling. He stalked down the hallway and ripped open the door to Mark's office.

Mark jolted backward in his chair, eyes wide in surprise. "Geez, Toby. You could've knocked."

"I never realized you were such a vindictive little bitch." Toby stormed up to his desk and leaned across with an accusatory finger jabbed into Mark's chest. "You got Merrick fired."

Scooting back his chair, Mark's brow furrowed. "I don't know what you're talking about." The slight smirk edging the corners of his mouth belied his denial.

Trembling with rage, Toby slammed his palms onto the desk. "You complained about him kissing me." The words sizzled through his clenched teeth.

Mark crossed his arms over his chest. "Yes, I did. But I didn't think he'd get fired over that."

"Liar!" The word roared out.

"What the hell is going on in here?"

Toby swung around and glared at Marsha standing in the doorway. "Your buddy here got the concierge fired."

She glared at Toby. "I don't care what you think he did to your little friend. You will speak to my employees with respect."

He barked out a laugh at her. "That's rich coming from you." He leveled his gaze on each of them then turned his wrath onto Marsha. "You two make quite a pair." He swung his glare back to Mark. "The traitor." And then at Marsha. "And his blind executioner."

Without another word, Toby stalked past Marsha and stormed to his office. Slamming the door, he pressed his back against it and let his head bump against the smooth wood. *Fuck.*

AT FIVE O'CLOCK, he powered down his computer. No one had knocked on his door for the entire afternoon, and he'd made no effort to reach out to anyone. He'd even kept his e-mail closed.

Grabbing his coat off the hook on the wall, he cracked open the door and peeked out. The hallway was completely quiet, and all of the office doors were open with lights off. He cautiously edged down the hallway, ready to bolt if anyone popped out at him.

Roger's office was dark, as was Herrington's, Marsha's, and Mark's. He breathed a sigh of relief, increasing his pace and reaching the reception area. A glance at the board told him he was the last one there. Marsha's name had a note next to it: *offsite in AM*.

Pushing his marker to OUT, Toby opened the door and strode to the elevator. He took the carriage down to the parking garage level, his nerves completely shot as he tried to figure out what he could say to Merrick.

The click of his dress shoes echoed around the concrete of the garage as he hurried to his car and got in. He started the engine and pulled out into traffic.

Guilt burned a hole in his gut. It was his fault Merrick had lost his job. The traffic inched along Fifth. Instead of turning onto Columbia, he continued south, taking the surface streets down to First and onto the West Seattle Bridge.

As he crested the top of the bridge, his phone dinged. Fishing it from his pocket, he glanced at the message.

At your pub. Vicky's taking care of me. I'll be waiting for you. A heart emoticon ended the message.

Some relief settled onto him. If Merrick was angry, he wouldn't have trekked all the way back to West Seattle after going home.

He continued past the steel mill, mulling Merrick's predicament as well as his own. Merrick could easily get another job, maybe go and finish school and make much more than Toby ever dreamed possible.

However, Toby's own situation needed more careful consideration. If he left Herrington, Fisher, and Scallione, would he be able to get another job? He'd be asked in the next interview why he'd left this position after only a short time with a two-year gap in his employment. The image of a hypothetical hiring manager glaring down her nose as he explained that his ex-boyfriend had shown up and he couldn't stomach staying played across his mind.

As he turned up Alaska Street, his stomach rumbled, pulling him out of his musings. He realized it had been over six hours since he'd eaten the teriyaki with Stazi. She was right, as usual. None of this was worth being miserable.

He found a parking spot three doors away from the pub and pulled the Mini into the tight space. After locking the car, he hurried to the entrance and pushed open the door. Just entering the restaurant lowered his anxiety. This was the one place where his problems didn't matter, and he could clear his head while being doted on by the waitstaff.

Christine hustled up to him. "Hey, Toby. Glad to see you." She aimed her gaze at the booths. "I put Merrick in the last one by the stairs."

"Thanks, Christine. We've both had a rough day." He headed down the aisle between booths and chairs.

Merrick jumped up and pulled him in close for a hug.

"Hey, handsome."

Nuzzling his forehead into Merrick's chest, Toby wrapped his arms around the thin waist. "I'm so sorry," he said, his voice husky with emotion.

"Don't be. It isn't your fault." He kissed the top of Toby's head. "I should have known better, but I wanted that asshole to know you're mine."

Reluctant to let go, Toby shook his head. "It *is* my fault. Mark was looking for revenge. I'd ripped him a new one at the corner a few minutes before, and I'm sure it added insult to injury to see me kissing someone else."

Without ending the embrace, Merrick edged back so he could look into Toby's eyes. "I *wanted* to kiss you, and that's on me." His eyebrow wriggled. "I want to kiss you right now, too."

Vicky strode by. "Go ahead, boys. No one will complain here."

Still holding onto each other, they burst into laughter.

Locking his gaze on Toby, Merrick tilted up Toby's chin and kissed him. When he drew back, his breaths were coming faster. "We should probably sit down."

Stepping back, Merrick waited for Toby to slide into the bench seat before taking the other and facing him across the table.

"Shit, Merrick. What are you going to do?" Toby shook his head. "This is a nightmare."

He shrugged. "Nah. I've got plenty of cash to tide me over until I regroup and find another job. I'll start looking next week. What about you?"

"Stazi told me nothing was worth being miserable, but

I don't know if I can find another job. It took me two years to get this one." He propped an elbow on the table and set the side of his head on his open palm.

"She's right, you know." Merrick reached across and took Toby's hand, pulling it away from his face.

The grip radiated comfort and strength. Their fingers intertwined, and a gentle smile accompanied the softening of Merrick's eyes.

Toby sighed as he melted into Merrick's gaze. "You really know how to calm me down."

"I'm glad to help." His thumb rubbed over the top of Toby's hand. "If you can't find something right away, you can let your apartment go and stay with me."

Toby tried to pull back, but Merrick didn't let go. "I couldn't ask that of you."

"Who's asking? I'm offering." Merrick gave Toby's hand a squeeze. "I've fallen hard for you, and I don't want to lose the chance to explore this relationship before it's even gotten started."

A heat of both embarrassment and desire for Merrick burned across his cheeks. "I feel the same way." He chuckled. "Your wooing worked."

Merrick pulled Toby's hand to his lips and placed two kisses on the back. "I'll show you later how much I want you."

Vicky sidled up to the table. "Sorry to interrupt, dears. Can I get you anything?"

Clearing his throat, Toby gently extracted his hand from Merrick's grip. "I could use a beer. The Pilsner."

She turned to Merrick "How about you, hun?"

"Hard cider, please."

"Anything to eat while I'm here?" She pulled out a pad and wrote the drink orders.

Toby flipped open a menu then glanced up at Merrick. "Dinner or some appetizers?"

"Appetizers sounds good." He sat back. "You choose."

Arching an eyebrow, Toby scanned the list. "Okay, sweet potato fries, the hummus plate…" He glanced at Merrick. "Artichoke dip okay with you, or should we do the wings?"

Merrick shrugged. "Both."

Toby laughed. "Okay, both."

"Sounds good, guys." She turned and hustled toward the bar.

Merrick reached across the table and took Toby's hand again, his brow wrinkled. "Tell me what happened this afternoon at the office."

Toby recounted walking in to overhear the explosive argument between the three partners. Then the interaction with Mark and Marsha, after he'd learned of Merrick's firing, came tumbling out.

Chuckling, Merrick gripped his hand tighter. "Did you really call him a vindictive little bitch?"

A smile tugged at the corners of Toby's mouth. "Yeah. And he definitely is one."

"Full points for subtlety." Merrick's thumb continued to trace patterns on his palm. "So, you explosively took down both Mark and Marsha."

"I don't know if I took them down. Probably more likely, I just signed my unemployment check." Maybe he would have to move in with Merrick. Stazi didn't have room for him for more than a week, and he couldn't bear moving back to his parents' place.

One step at a time.

Vicky brought over their drinks and set them on the table. "Food's coming right up."

After she'd left them alone again, Merrick raised his pint. "To us. May the universe do the right thing and give us both a break."

Toby clinked his glass with Merrick's. "I'll drink to that."

They both took a sip and set their pints back on the table as Vicky delivered the hummus plate and the artichoke dip. Christine brought the fries and wings a moment later.

"You guys need anything else?" Christine asked.

Toby shook his head. "This looks great."

"Enjoy." She smiled and headed back to the front of the pub.

After dragging a round of cucumber through the hummus, Toby popped the morsel into his mouth. Merrick snagged a wing and went to work on it.

Finishing his bite, Toby dabbed the corners of his mouth with a napkin. "What do you think I should do about the job?"

Merrick set the bone on his plate. "That's completely up to you. I know you're a capable guy. Like I said, I'm hot for a man who has it all together."

With a snort, Toby concentrated on dragging another cucumber through the hummus. "I feel like a lot is falling apart right now."

"Hey."

Toby looked up.

Merrick fixed him with an intense stare. "You're going to be fine. It might take a little time, but I know it's all going to work out." He wiped off his hands with his napkin. "Give me your hand."

Keeping his eyes on Merrick's, Toby reached across the table. "Now what?"

With a firm grasp, Merrick held tight. "Remember when we first met? I told you I'm the luckiest person my friends know."

"I remember." Toby breathed as the same spark and crackle of electricity made his entire body tingle at their connection.

Merrick lifted his hand and kissed it. "For extra luck. Tomorrow, either way you decide or if fate decides for you, I know it will be what's right."

"Do you believe in magic?" Toby asked as Merrick released his hand.

"As a matter of fact, I do." He winked. "I also believe in luck, which is likely the same thing."

Toby leaned forward. "The luckiest thing that's happened to me in a long time was meeting you."

With a huge smile, Merrick picked up a carrot stick. "I'm the fortunate one. Luck brought me to you."

"Let's finish up here and head back to my place." He arched his eyebrow. "You *are* staying with me tonight, right?"

"Definitely." Merrick popped the carrot into his mouth.

★ ★ ★

TOBY PUSHED OPEN his apartment door and held it for Merrick. After they both stepped inside, Toby hesitated by the entrance to the kitchen. "Can I get you anything?" He grinned. "I don't think I have any pie."

Merrick laughed. "I have a confession. There wasn't any pie at my place either. Thankfully, that wasn't the dessert you wanted last night."

"To think, my virtue stolen on the ruse of pie." He closed the distance between them and stood in front of Merrick. "How about you get settled in the bedroom. I need to run to the restroom before I join you."

"Sounds wonderful." Merrick kissed him, giving him a squeeze before trotting into the bedroom.

Goosebumps spread across Toby's back at the sensations from the brief kiss. He hurried into the bathroom, brushed his teeth, and relieved himself. Eager to rejoin Merrick, he washed his face and let his hands soak up the warmth of the water before shutting off the faucet and drying them.

He flipped off the bathroom light, closed the blinds in the living room, checked that the door was securely locked, and headed to the bedroom. The sight that greeted him brought Toby to a full halt, his mouth salivating. Merrick lay completely naked and stroked his impressive dick, a grin arching across his lips, and his blue eyes blazing with desire.

Closing the door behind him, Toby hurried into the room and ripped his clothes off. As he stripped, he raked his gaze over Merrick's lean body. Some might think

Merrick too thin, but Toby loved his lines and the sweet dusting of hair on his flat chest.

Slipping off his briefs and socks, Toby stood naked before Merrick.

Merrick squeezed his cock as a whistle escaped his lips. "I'll never get tired of looking at your beauty."

Heat whipped across Toby's cheeks while his dick hardened. "I feel the same way about you."

Now, Merrick blushed. "I'm nothing compared to you."

Flicking off the light, Toby crossed to the futon and clicked on the bedside lamp. He climbed in and lay his head on Merrick's chest.

Toby traced his fingers along the outline of ribs and across the flatness of Merrick's stomach. "I think you're perfect. Thank you for staying the night with me."

Merrick's hand lightly rubbed across Toby's back, making him moan at the tender caress. Kissing Merrick's chest, Toby maneuvered himself on top of Merrick and stared into his sultry blue eyes.

Reaching up, Merrick cupped Toby's cheek and pulled him close. Their erections rubbed against each other's as their lips molded together, eliciting more moans from both men.

Toby planted his hands on either side of Merrick's chest and pushed himself up, then used his knees to spread Merrick's legs apart. Merrick wrapped them around Toby's waist, resting his heels on Toby's ass.

Merrick's hands traveled from Toby's stomach up to his chest and tweaked the nipples, sending a shockwave of sensation through his body and making his cock strain.

"I want you inside of me, Toby. Please."

This evening was about deepening their connection, and Toby had no intention of a quick fuck. He wanted this to last.

Leaning down, he ground his dick against Merrick's groin and planted another deep kiss. His tongue probed against Merrick's lips and gained entry, tenderly touching his tongue and thoroughly exploring every nook and cranny of his mouth.

With his hands gliding all over Toby, Merrick deepened the intensity of the kiss. Toby allowed himself to lay more heavily on top of Merrick, savoring every point their skin connected. Merrick increased the strength of his embrace, pulling Toby in even tighter.

Finally, Toby needed a moment to regroup as his balls started to tingle and his cock hardened to the point he feared he'd shoot. "Hold on, I need a minute, or this will end too soon." He pushed himself up, and Merrick released the hold his legs had around Toby's waist.

"Everything you're doing to me has me on the edge of coming," Merrick whispered, then rubbed his hand down Toby's ribs to his hips.

Each tender caress made Toby want Merrick more. He couldn't believe he'd fallen so hard for this man, and it seemed Merrick felt the same way. Toby reached over Merrick's head to the night stand and opened a drawer. He pulled out a condom and some lubricant, hoping the rubbers weren't too old to use. He checked the date on them and was relieved to see they hadn't passed the expiration stamped into the foil packaging.

"What were you looking at?" Merrick kissed his chest.

"Just making sure it's still good." He set the package on the floor then pushed Merrick's legs up. He poured a dollop of lube onto his index finger.

Merrick hugged his knees to his chest. "Get me ready. Might take a couple fingers to open me up. It's been a long time since I've had anyone inside me."

"For me, too. Mark was the last man I did anything with besides you, and we were safe." He pressed his finger against the puckered opening and carefully slicked around the entrance. Applying more pressure, he worked his way into the gripping chute and slowly pushed and pulled.

From his moans and gasps, Merrick seemed to enjoy what Toby was doing. When Toby's finger tapped against the hard nub, Merrick's eyes shot open, and he let out a long moan. "Oh, God, Toby." His hole gripped tightly around the invading finger. "Amazing."

Toby slipped his finger out briefly to apply more lube as well as to slick his middle finger. "Ready for a second one?"

Nodding, Merrick spread his cheeks wide.

Toby slowly pressed two fingers into the tender opening, gently stretching the tightly gripping muscles as he went.

Merrick clutched the sheets, and his head thrashed from side to side.

Frowning, Toby inched his fingers back toward the entrance. "Too much?"

"No!" Merrick yelled. "Please don't stop."

With a grin and a pulse of his cock, Toby pressed his digits deeper, prodding Merrick's prostate. Merrick's legs spread as he impaled himself deeper with Toby's fingers. The hardness between his legs leaked onto his abdomen and gave a little jump with each deep prod.

Toby continued to work Merrick while he drizzled the lube over the young man's stiff shaft. After tossing the bottle onto the floor, he pressed his palm along the slick erection and wrapped his hand around the leaking head.

Grabbing Toby's wrist, Merrick stared into his eyes. "You'll make me shoot."

Toby squeezed, feeling a jolt as he prodded Merrick's prostate at the same time. His own cock jumped at the way Merrick's gaze pleaded with Toby.

"I don't want to come until you do." Merrick wrenched Toby's hand from the head of his prick. "I'm ready. Slide inside me."

Needing no further encouragement, Toby snatched the condom from the floor and ripped open the packaging. He rolled the rubber down his shaft, then applied more of the lube to Merrick's ass and the sheath over his cock. He lined up, locked his gaze with Merrick's, and slid inside.

Merrick fought to keep his eyes open, but he held Toby's gaze while inch after thick inch of hard cock dipped inside him.

Once he'd reached the bottom of the shaft, Toby held still, savoring the velvety feel of Merrick's ass and concentrating on not shooting his load.

With a nod, Merrick gyrated his hole around Toby's cock. "Take me, Toby. I'm yours."

Toby rocked his hips forward and back, establishing a slow and gentle rhythm. He leaned forward, pressing his body against Merrick's, and again molded their lips together.

A gentle moan filled his mouth. Toby parted his lips and swiped his tongue inside. Merrick's hands pulled down on Toby's back, and he intensified the kiss.

Toby increased his thrusts into a rhythmic pounding while Merrick held on, breaking the kiss and leaning his head back into the pillow. "So close."

The light tingle in Toby's balls built as he neared his own release. He thrust forward, driving them both toward their orgasms.

Merrick's entire body tensed. "Toby!" He arched his back, and warmth spread between them with each throb of Merrick's cock against Toby's torso.

The gripping tightness of Merrick's chute rocketed Toby over the edge, and he loaded shot after shot into the rubber buried deep inside Merrick.

Clutching at each other as they both rode out their orgasms, Toby shuddered against Merrick's body. When the rush of their release subsided, Toby gently eased himself out of Merrick and slid sideways, still keeping half of his body over Merrick's.

One of Merrick's arms snaked around his shoulders, and Toby rested his head on Merrick's chest.

His lover drew and released a deep breath. "Did you feel that, Toby?"

With effort, Toby lifted his head. "Feel what?"

"I'm pretty sure the earth moved."

Chuckling, Toby returned his head to the warm skin and listened as Merrick's heart beat rapidly. They lay there for several moments, and Toby's eyes lulled as a wave of drowsiness crashed over him.

With a squeeze, Merrick nudged him. "Hey."

"Yeah?"

"How about we clean up? I'm a sticky mess." Merrick kissed the top of his head. "And you need to get rid of the condom."

Toby pushed himself up on shaky arms. Though a lot of the strength had been sapped from his body, so had the worry and anger he'd been feeling earlier.

Swinging his long legs off of the futon, Merrick stood and held out his hand. "Let me help you up."

When he grasped the outstretched hand, Merrick pulled him to his feet and into an embrace. "I'm crazy about you." He pressed his lips on Toby's while his hands drifted down to the condom still hugging the softened cock. Keeping their lips pressed tight, Merrick unrolled the rubber and then held their sticky, sweaty bodies together as he finished the kiss.

Once they broke away from each other, Toby took the spent rubber from Merrick. "That was hands down the sexiest way I've ever taken off a condom."

Merrick laughed. "By the feel of it, I'd say you filled it good. Let's get cleaned up. We have some serious snuggling still to do."

"I like the way you think." Toby led him to the bathroom and ran the water in the sink until it warmed. "Washcloths are in the cabinet by the door."

Merrick retrieved one while Toby tied off the condom and dropped it into the waste can. Taking the cloth, Toby soaked it in the sink and turned to Merrick. He ran the warm rag over Merrick's stomach and chest, then carefully cleaned off his cock. It chubbed in his hand as he thoroughly wiped away the stickiness.

"Turn around," Toby murmured.

Complying, Merrick braced his hands on the sink and leaned forward, jutting his ass at Toby. If he had brought another condom with him, they'd have gone another round. Merrick's entire body turned him on, but still, the best part was losing himself in those blue eyes.

He glanced up at the mirror to see Merrick studying him.

"Something wrong?" his lover asked.

"Not in the slightest." Toby ran the cloth around the cheeks and up the crack, carefully wiping away the remnants of their coupling. He gave the cheeks a gentle pat. "Nice and clean."

"You were very thorough." Merrick took the cloth from him and rinsed it in the sink. "Your turn."

Toby leaned his butt on the edge of the counter, presenting the front of his body to Merrick. The tenderness of the caresses with the washcloth that Merrick lavished on him took his breath away.

Merrick chuckled as he tossed the cloth onto the sink. "You seem to have a problem there."

Grabbing his fully erect dick, Toby gave it a couple strokes. "Nothing you can't handle."

"Whoa, cowboy. You are probably the gentlest lover

I've ever been with, but I need a little rest before we ride another rodeo." He pulled Toby away from the sink and into an embrace. "Come on, partner," he drawled. "Let's mosey into the bedroom and hit the hay."

Holding hands, Toby followed along as Merrick led them back to the futon. He kissed Toby's hand then peered at the small mattress.

Sidling up next to Merrick, Toby pressed against his body. "I guess you could sleep with your knees pressed to your chest."

Merrick chuckled. "I might have to." With a sideways glance at Toby, he shook his head. "No, I can fit. You don't mind being held and cuddled all night, do you? I mean, I did it last night, but I didn't ask if you liked it."

Toby sat on the small wooden frame and patted the mattress next to him. "I loved it. The way you held me made my troubles melt away."

Merrick sat next to him and took his hand. "You know, I don't do this often. Sex, I mean. I don't just hop into bed with anyone." He kissed Toby's fingers as he interlaced them with his own.

Butterflies fluttered in Toby's chest, and he lay his head against Merrick's shoulder. "Why did you do it with me?"

"You're special." He squeezed Toby's hand. "I know we haven't known each other very long, but everything feels so right when I'm with you. I loved going to work knowing you're just upstairs." He chuckled. "Kissing you in the lobby felt so natural. I don't care if Mark got me fired for it. I'm glad he saw how much I've come to care about you."

Toby's breath caught in his throat as Merrick turned his head to nuzzle his nose in Toby's hair. He released Toby's hand and wrapped his arms around Toby.

Merrick continued. "I don't expect you feel the same way about me, but…"

Swiveling to lock his gaze on Merrick's, Toby lifted his hand to caress the stubble along Merrick's cheek. "I *do* feel the same way. You're such an amazing guy, and I feel so lucky to have found you. Like I said, Mark was the last guy I've been with, and there was only one before him. Stazi can tell you I haven't put myself out there very much, and after Mark hurt me so badly, I gave up."

"Yet you took a chance on me." He brought one hand around and held Toby's against his lips, kissing the palm.

"Even though you weren't the first in line?" Toby arched an eyebrow.

After a confused pause, Merrick realized what Toby meant. "Close enough, but I'm the one who's around."

"Without a place to…" Toby trailed off, staring at the floor. The misquoted song's meaning suddenly became very real. After tomorrow, he literally might have no place to go. Fired in the morning for popping off at Marsha.

"Hey." Merrick tapped Toby's chin and turned it back to face him. "ABBA songs aside, I'm here if you need me, whether it's to move in for a little bit, or just…" he winked, "…if you're feeling down."

In spite of his worries, Toby laughed. "You're the best."

"Come on, beautiful." Merrick folded himself onto the

small bed, his long legs hanging off the end. "Cuddle up with me, and we'll take tomorrow as it comes."

As Toby spooned against Merrick, he reached up and turned off the bedside lamp. After tugging the comforter over both of them, Merrick pushed one arm under the pillow and wrapped the other around Toby's chest.

Holding him close, Merrick planted small kisses along Toby's neck and shoulder. "Good night, sweet man."

The warmth and gentle pressure of Merrick's body relaxed Toby, but as sleep descended over him, he couldn't help worrying about what the morning would bring.

CHAPTER NINE

THE ALARM'S RENDITION of *Waterloo* was not a welcome sound at five-thirty in the morning. Toby pushed his eyes open and slowly became aware of a hard thickness pressing along the crevice of his ass.

Chuckling, he climbed out of Merrick's embrace and scrambled to turn off the music. His companion lightly snored, not awakened by the alarm. Toby padded across the floor and gently shut the bedroom door before heading into the bathroom and turning on the shower. As the water warmed, he relieved himself, then flushed and stepped into the shower stall.

The words of the song his alarm had randomly played wove through his mind, and he wondered if he was facing his Waterloo with Roger and Herrington. Fully aware that Marsha was on the warpath and looking for a reason to fire him, he'd foolishly exploded at Mark and Marsha—she had a willing witness. Even if she wasn't gunning for him, he'd committed a serious HR violation. Combined with the liability he'd already become to his bosses, Roger might have no alternative other than to let him go.

At least, he'd have Merrick to come home to.

After quickly washing himself, he shut off the shower

and ran the towel over his body. Life felt bearable after a hot shower. He wiped off the mirror with the towel and cracked the door open.

As he brushed his teeth, Merrick tapped his fingers on the door. "Mind if I join you?"

Toby paused, his mouth full of foaming toothpaste. "Come on in."

"Are you okay?" Merrick's brow furrowed. "You seem to be foaming at the mouth."

With a laugh, Toby spit out the toothpaste. "Funny guy."

"I'm a riot in the morning." Wearing a smirk and nothing else, he stepped closer and snaked his arms around Toby's body, tracing the hair along his balls with his fingertips.

Toby sighed, tingles of pleasure radiating from his groin. "You know, I do have to go to work."

"Are you sure?" Not ceasing his fondling, Merrick planted kisses along Toby's shoulder, increasing the tingles and weakening his resolve.

"Not really sure, but I probably should. I don't want to give them even more reason to fire me." He leaned forward, his ass pushing against Merrick's morning erection, and rinsed out his mouth.

"I wish you could stay." Merrick took full advantage, sliding his shaft between Toby's cheeks and raking his fingers lightly down Toby's spine. A second wave of tingles exploded in the wake of his touch.

With a sigh, Toby straightened and closed his eyes for a moment as Merrick ground against him and trailed his fingers over Toby's shoulders and across his pecs.

"I know you have to go." He kissed along Toby's neck. "But, whatever happens today, know I'll be here ready to do anything you want when you get home." He nibbled on Toby's earlobe and whispered. "Anything."

Toby's cock leapt, and his body shuddered at the sensuous treatment Merrick gave him. His knees shook, and he reached out to steady himself on the sink.

Chuckling, Merrick stepped back, and Toby immediately missed his touch and the warmth his body radiated. "Do you have breakfast fixings in the fridge?"

Toby glanced up into the mirror. "Yeah," he gasped.

"I'll make you something before you go." He left the bathroom with a mischievous grin.

Toby sagged against the sink, a smile stretching his mouth. Merrick had known exactly what he was doing. He'd be a walking hard-on all morning.

TOBY TOOK A tentative step into the reception area and glanced at Elsibeth. She smiled warmly. "Good morning, Toby."

"Uh, hi. Do I still have a job here?" He stood at the counter in front of her desk.

"Last I checked. Your name is still on the board, so I'm guessing yes." She nodded at the board. "You'd better sign in."

He stepped to the wall and pushed the token by his name to IN. Looking over the names, Marsha was out at her offsite meeting; Roger was here; Herrington and

Angelica were in meetings; and Mark wasn't in yet. Several others were already here, but these were the folks pertinent to his predicament.

Returning to the desk, he slipped off his coat and held it in his hand. "Elsibeth, can I ask you something?"

"Of course." She took the headpiece out of her ear and set it on the desk. "Fire away."

His nerves flared. "Are you aware of what's going on with me and Mark?"

She winced. "Yes. Anyone with ears has heard all the yelling in the last few days." She leaned forward. "Marsha said something about financial improprieties at your last job, but Herrington shut her down really fast. Unless she has proof, he told her to not bring it up again."

Toby tore his gaze away from hers. As he feared, everyone in the office knew what had gone down at Teller Electronics. He couldn't stay here.

She cleared her throat. "Toby?"

"Sorry, what?" He brought his gaze back to her.

"When you sit at a reception desk, you develop a good intuition about the character of the people who come and go from the office." She hardened her gaze. "From what I can tell, you're a good person. Unless you've got me completely snowed, and I doubt that because you seem to wear your heart on your sleeve. I don't believe what Marsha's saying."

"Thanks. I should get to work." He turned to head down the hallway to his office. Despite her words, he'd made up his mind.

"Toby, one last thing."

He stopped but didn't look at her. "Yes?"

"Marsha, for her faults, must have some doubts as well, or she wouldn't be investigating."

Spinning around to face her, his stomach tightened. "What?"

Elsibeth kept her gaze steady. "The offsite is a meeting with the marketing folks at Teller Electronics."

"They're the ones who made all the accusations against me." He shook his head, his initial panic giving way to reluctant acceptance of his fate. "Oh, well. Thanks for telling me." He turned and trudged away. Pausing at the copy room, he glanced at the supply cabinet. A couple of empty paper boxes were stacked next to the recycle bin. He grabbed one and strode to his office.

Roger waited in one of the chairs next to his desk. "Good morning." He eyed the box and crossed his arms. "What's that for?"

With a sigh, Toby entered the office and hung his jacket on the hook. He brought the box to his desk and set it down, then sat in the chair next to Roger. "Marsha is meeting my former employer, getting Mark's story corroborated by the other marketing folks there." He ran his hands over his eyes and pulled them down his cheeks. "This has gotten untenable. They're not going to defend me. In fact, they're the ones who leveled the first accusations even before the transfers were discovered."

Roger puffed out a breath. "Herrington and I have complete faith in you. Marsha can't touch you."

"No, but she can make my life miserable. As my best friend told me at lunch yesterday, nothing's worth being miserable." He sagged in the seat. "And I've already ended up hurting Merrick."

Roger's eyes widened. "Did he dump you?"

A smile tugged at his lips. "He doubled down on how much he wants us to be together. My past is what got him fired, though. Mark complained about a kiss, and Merrick lost his job."

"Fucking asshole." With his brow furrowed, Roger spat out the words. He sighed. "Is there anything I can do to get you to stay?"

"Other than finding some magical way to clear my name, I don't think so." Toby rose and went to his desk.

Roger stood and leaned his hands on the tabletop. "Could I at least ask you to stay for the rest of the day and help me with a few things before you go? I'll ask Herrington if we can give you a bonus for all the work you've already done. We'd be dead in the water without you."

With a nod, Toby sank into his desk chair. "Sure, I'd be happy to help you."

Moving to the door, Roger gave Toby a last look. "I've e-mailed a couple of projects to you. Let me know if you can get them finished before you go."

Toby powered on his computer, grateful to have something to do. "Thanks, Roger. I'll come see you before I leave."

"Damn it, Toby. I'm very sorry to see you go." He strode out the door and headed down the hallway.

The next few hours passed quickly as Toby tried to get through the list of things Roger had sent. By two-thirty, he'd finished the majority of the tasks and felt Roger could handle the rest.

Just before he was going to power down his computer, an e-mail from Marsha appeared. The preview window displayed the message.

Tobias,
I'd like to see you in my office.
M

He fired back a note to her:

You win. I'm leaving. No need to meet.

After hitting send, he put together his things and stacked them in the box. The box was only half full, but he was glad not to awkwardly carry his personal effects for the walk of shame down the hall and out the door. He grabbed his coat from the hook and laid it across the top of the box. Then he turned to the door, intending to report to Roger for the last time.

"Where do you think you're going?"

CHAPTER TEN

RED-FACED UNDER HER straw-colored hair, Marsha stood in his doorway, surveying first Toby and then the box on his desk. "Before you do anything hasty, I'd like to see you in my office. Now."

He frowned at her, no longer caring what she thought. "What do you think you possibly have to say to me?"

"Come find out." She steamed down the hall without another word.

Contemplating just picking up his box and walking away, he paused as something niggled at the back of his mind. She was angry. Red-in-the-face angry. And was that a tinge of embarrassment? Shouldn't she be happy? Some smug little comment and a happy dance at his door as he left? And she'd said *before you do* any*thing hasty…*

Curiosity overrode his anger and misgivings. He warily moved along the hallway and hovered at the doorway to Marsha's office. She stood behind her desk, silent and glaring at a visibly confused Mark.

She glanced up at Toby. "Come in and have a seat." Though her tone wasn't welcoming in the slightest, he didn't detect the distain she usually displayed for him.

Without a word, he entered the office, taking the chair

next to his former boyfriend and crossing his arms.

Mark glanced at him, furrowed his brow, and turned to his boss. "What's going on, Marsha? I thought he was leaving."

"I'll bet you couldn't wait." Her nostrils flared. "I had a very interesting conversation this morning with Abel Flerchinger."

Toby cocked his head to the side. Abel was the Marketing Director at Teller Electronics. The one who'd insisted he be terminated when they'd discovered the money was being syphoned off. Toby kept his mouth shut, waiting for Marsha to continue.

Mark, on the other hand, spluttered next to him with his face as white as a sheet. "Y-you did?"

Her eyes narrowed, piercing the squirming man with her glare. "*Yes. I. Did.* Do you have something to say to me, or more importantly, to Tobias, here?"

This was getting surreal. *She's angry at Mark over something Abel had said?* Though he loathed even looking at his former boyfriend, Toby stared at him.

Mark shrank in his seat. "There's nothing to tell," he said, his voice unusually small and weak. "Toby transferred that money like I told you—"

Slapping her hand on her desk, her glare bore into Mark. "Sabrina Michaelson confessed."

Toby sat up in his seat and stared at Marsha. "Confessed to what?" He turned again to the man shaking in the seat next to him. "Mark Logan Spencer, what have you done to me now?"

"Oh, God." He faced Toby, fear evident in his eyes. "I

lied."

With a snort, Toby sat back and crossed his arms again. "That's nothing new."

"No, Toby. I *really* lied." He tore his gaze away, fear changing to shame. "Not just about those guys on the side or that I didn't eat the last of your favorite chocolates."

Toby's brow furrowed, and his stomach sank. "Then what?"

Mark took a deep breath and sighed again. "About your involvement in the money-laundering operation." He briefly glanced at Toby before fixing his gaze firmly on his hands in his lap. "I set up a camera in your office to get your login and password to the bank, and then I stole your fob while you were asleep and gave it to Sabrina."

A gasp escaped Toby's lips. The missing fob. The smoking gun, so to speak—the reason he'd been asked to resign.

Mark continued, his head still hanging. "Sabrina and Ken Haught hatched some plan that involved moving cash, but I didn't really know what it was about. I thought they were transferring money to a Marketing account to supplement what they had in their budget."

Marsha, who'd been uncharacteristically quiet during Mark's explanation, piped up. "And what happened next? That's not the end of the story."

With a gulp, Mark nodded. "Abel found out about the money transfer, but Sabrina convinced him you were behind the whole thing. I didn't know all the details until Ken threatened me. They said if they went down, I'd go to jail with them. I freaked out. That's why you came home to a mostly empty house. I left because I couldn't stand what I'd done to you, but if I'd come clean, I'd have gone to prison."

"*You. Rotten. Bastard.*" Toby's voice rose in pitch and volume with each word. Pure fury replaced the curiosity that had brought him to Marsha's office and the shock of discovering what Sabrina and Ken had done. "Are you fucking kidding me with this? Do you have *any* idea what I've lost because of you?"

Beneath Toby's furious glare, Mark squirmed and sank further into his seat. "Look, I made a mistake, and I was scared. I didn't really know what those people were doing until it was too late." He glanced at Toby and frowned. "And then I made it worse by throwing you under the bus, corroborating Sabrina and Ken's story."

"Oh, and don't you dare forget stealing my grandma's table and my fucking rocking chair, cleaning me out after taking my job away." Toby was nearly shouting. "I lost my home and almost every friend I had because of you!"

"And you're damned right you made a mistake," Marsha ground out. The fury emanating from her lit up the room with hostile energy, but for a change it wasn't focused on Toby. "I've been riding this guy since the minute he got here because of your lies, but apparently, I didn't know the half of it."

She glared at Mark, making Toby's former boyfriend wince.

"I'm sorry, Toby," Mark said. "Really, I don't have enough words to say how much I regret what I put you through."

Not giving Mark an inch, Toby turned away. Nothing the man could say would make up for the torment and the loss he'd caused.

Marsha continued, the words sizzling across the desk. "You're only sorry you got caught. If you'd had any remorse, you'd have come clean. Now that I have the full story, I'm going to do two things. First, Spencer, you're fired. Get your things and leave. *Now.*"

Mark hung his head and rose. He started to say something, but clamped his mouth shut and shuffled toward the exit.

Before he made it to the door, Marsha swung her gaze to Toby. "Second, Tobias, I'm giving you a raise, and I'll pay for it out of my own budget. You'll get the remainder of what I was paying him."

Toby sat back in the chair, wide-eyed and staring at the person he'd assumed was his enemy. "I don't know what to say."

Remorse shone in the steely depths of her stare. "Say you'll stay. I have a lot to make up for." She flicked her gaze back to Mark. "Why are you still in my office?"

He turned his back on her and fled the room.

Taking her seat, Marsha fixed Toby with a friendly smile, though her eyes still blazed. "That little shit will never work in this town again. If he gives you any trouble whatsoever, come and tell me, and I'll make sure his life is hell."

Still unsure what to do with this strange turn of events, Toby shifted in his seat. "Uh, thanks."

"Now, I have some paperwork to get to Roger for your

raise. I'm sure Billy won't mind. You'll get another twenty thousand for this budget year to make up for my idiocy and lack of research. Next year, we'll see how it goes, but we'll increase your salary at the very minimum by ten thousand. How does that sound?"

His mind still whirling, Toby realized his mouth had dropped open and closed it. "I, uh. Wow, thank you." He rose. "I should get back to work. Um, thank you."

She nodded. "Don't mention it. Drop by any time you want a chat, and I mean it...if Spencer gives you any trouble..." She clenched her fist.

Turning, Toby nearly tripped over the chair as he headed to the door.

"Oh, and I spoke to the concierge manager. Young Merrick should be getting a call." He heard her pick up her phone and the beep of the button calling reception. "Elsibeth, Marsha here. Spencer is leaving. If he's not out in the next ten minutes, call security and have him tossed out on his ass."

Toby nearly stumbled down the hallway, his heart pounding in his chest as he struggled to grasp what had just happened. Wielding the second box that had been in the copier room, Mark stepped out of his office and stopped. His cheeks turned bright red, and he dropped his gaze to the floor.

"I'll, uh, have your stuff delivered to you."

Stepping past him, Toby continued on and didn't look back. Mark was part of his history, a dark chapter that had firmly and forever closed. The nightmare was over, and he could finally think about the future.

Roger and Herrington were waiting for him when he arrived at his office. The hastily packed box still sat on his desk with his jacket draped over it. A vase with a dozen roses also stood on the desk.

"This was delivered while you were in with Marsha." Herrington stepped forward. "I have no idea what just happened, son. Are you all right?"

Toby blinked and shook his head. "Honestly, I'm still reeling. Marsha went to Teller this morning and got the real perpetrators of the money laundering to confess. I don't know how, but she can be intimidating…" Toby moved to the chair closest to the door and sat. "She cleared my name, fired Mark, and gave me a raise."

Herrington's eyebrows shot up. "A raise?"

Nodding, Toby still felt the numb shock gripping him. "From her budget."

Roger sat on the corner of Toby's desk facing him. "Does that mean you're staying?"

Toby nodded again. "Yeah, that is, if you want me to."

Pumping a fist in the air, Roger let out a whoop. "You bet we do."

Herrington smiled. "I'm glad this worked out. You'd have been difficult to replace." He nodded to both men and left the office.

"Need help unpacking?" Roger eyed the box on Toby's desk.

His energy and excitement reminded Toby of a child receiving the present he'd always wanted. With a chuckle, Toby shook his head. "I think I can handle it." He glanced at the vase. "Where did those come from?"

Roger plucked the card from the bouquet and handed it to Toby. "I can guess, but you should read the note."

Toby used a finger to pry open the seal and lifted out a small card.

Toby,

No matter what you decide today, I support you. Tonight, dinner is on me. I got my job back.

Love, Merrick

Toby's eyes widened as he stared at Roger. "Holy shit. Merrick's back at the concierge desk."

A grin spread across Roger's lips. "How about you take the rest of the afternoon off? There's only a couple hours left of the week anyway, and maybe you and Merrick can make some plans for the long weekend."

"Thanks, Roger. I really appreciate it." Toby moved around the desk and picked up the roses. "I'd better take these home. They'll wilt by Tuesday."

Roger hopped off of the desk and headed for the door. "Have a great weekend, and I will definitely see you bright and early Tuesday morning."

Grabbing his coat, Toby flicked off the light and hurried to the reception area to mark himself out.

Elsibeth rose from her desk and approached him. The older woman patted his shoulder. "I'm so glad you're staying."

"Me, too." He smiled at her. "Thanks for being so kind to me."

"I knew that Mark guy was trouble the minute he walked in here." She snorted. "Good riddance."

Toby chuckled. "You're telling me."

She nodded at the flowers. "Go give that young man a big hug and a kiss."

His chuckle turned to a laugh. "I intend to. See you Tuesday."

Toby strode from the reception area and caught the elevator to the lobby of the building. The doors opened, and he discovered Merrick back at his concierge desk beaming at the passing businessmen. He strode from the elevator bay to the desk. "Hey there, handsome. I hear you're back at work." Toby brandished the roses. "Where are we going to dinner?"

Merrick pushed off his chair and wrapped Toby in an embrace. "Anywhere you want."

Clutching the vase in one hand, Toby wrapped an arm around Merrick. "How about the pub in West Seattle? I can run these home, get changed, then meet you there."

Merrick stepped back and kept a hand on Toby's shoulder. "Sounds perfect."

The megawatt-smile on his face made Toby want to kiss him. But that hadn't ended so well the last time. "I'd better go before I do something completely inappropriate here in the lobby again." He took Merrick's hand and gave it a squeeze. "See you in a couple of hours?"

"Sure thing." The younger man checked his watch. "I'm off at four, and it'll take me about forty minutes to get over there."

Toby let go and moved toward the exit. "See you soon." He left the building and strode to his Mini in the parking garage. Pulling out onto University Street, he turned right on Fifth Avenue and headed to Columbia and the Viaduct.

The late afternoon sun shone brilliantly over Elliott Bay. Traffic inched along, but Toby didn't care. He had a date with someone he adored, a raise, and a bouquet of roses. Life was finally good.

EPILOGUE

TOBY LOGGED OFF his computer and stretched his
arms. With the long week finished, and three days of
vacation tacked onto the weekend, he could hardly contain
his excitement.

He fumbled for his phone as it dinged, and a text from
Stazi flashed on the screen.

One year today w/ M?

Smiling, he unlocked the screen and replied.

Yup. Dinner tonight. Champagne, depending. Well,
maybe prosecco. It was an Italian restaurant after all.

Four emoticons appeared. The first a face with its
mouth a perfect O, the second with its eyes bulging, the
third blowing him a kiss with a little heart, and the fourth
a four-leafed clover.

He smiled. *Will let you know how it goes.* He pocketed
the cell and stared at the roses on his desk. They'd been
delivered earlier that morning, and the card from Merrick
was every bit as sweet as the candy hearts on Elsibeth's
desk. He rose and grabbed his coat as Roger paused at the
entrance of his office.

"Hey, Toby. I'm heading off. Enjoy the weekend."

"Will do. I'm back on Thursday." He lifted the vase
off the desk and carried it to the door.

"You should have taken the whole week off." Eyeing the roses, Roger stepped aside while Toby flicked the light switch, and they walked to the reception area.

"Five days away is enough. Besides, Merrick didn't have that much time off." Toby set the vase on the reception desk and marked himself out, noting the day he'd be back in the office.

Roger did the same and opened the main door. "Well, have a good time away." He stepped out into the hallway and let the door shut.

Moving to the candy dish on Elsibeth's desk, he stared at the little hearts and spied the particular one he was hoping to find. After plucking it from the dish, he left the office and caught the elevator to the lobby.

Merrick was just slipping his coat on when Toby arrived at the concierge desk. "Good evening, sir." His lips curved into a grin.

"Hello, handsome. I have something for you." He handed the candy to Merrick.

The smile on his face broadened. "*I'm yours.* You remembered."

"Of course, I did." He hugged Merrick, tilting his head back to receive a quick kiss.

"You've been very mysterious about our Valentine's Day dinner. Where are we going?" Merrick released him from his embrace, and they headed for the swinging door.

The box in Toby's jacket pocket felt heavy as he stuck a hand inside and nervously fidgeted with the small, felt-covered container. "I made a reservation at a little Italian restaurant in West Seattle." He led his boyfriend to the

Mini, and they got in.

Merrick placed his hand on Toby's thigh. "Sounds perfect. I thought you were going to just take me to the pub. That's where it all started after all."

Toby shrugged nonchalantly, while inside his heart pounded with excitement. "I considered it but thought we'd want something a little more intimate. The girls would want to chat with us, and I want you all to myself." He put the car in gear and steered it around the pillars in the parking garage to the exit.

"What? A romantic restaurant on Valentine's Day?" Merrick chuckled. "Could it be that I finally got you to realize what a wonderful day it actually is?"

With a little smirk, Toby gave him a quick glance before he pulled out into traffic. "I'll let you be the judge of that."

Merrick rubbed his leg the entire way to the restaurant, making Toby reconsider going to dinner. He would rather have taken Merrick home, but he had special plans and wanted to give his boyfriend the full treatment the special day called for. Depending on how this went, the fun could wait.

Parking the car in front of the post office, Toby jumped out of the Mini and opened Merrick's door for him. He held out his hand as the tall man unfolded himself from the tiny car. After locking the doors, he held his boyfriend's hand while they strolled to the corner and crossed the street. Toby held the restaurant door open for Merrick and followed him inside.

"The lease is up on your apartment next month, isn't it?" Toby asked as they were seated at a small table in the back corner of the restaurant.

The waiter brought over two glasses and a bottle of wine, showing it to Merrick.

Raising an eyebrow, Merrick gave Toby a quizzical stare before nodding at the younger server. After sampling the wine, Merrick nodded again, and the waiter poured two glasses.

"Um, yeah, the lease is up. I wasn't sure about renewing." He leaned forward with a frown, lowering his voice to a whisper. "Toby, that's a very expensive bottle of wine."

Toby gave another shrug, but his heartbeat quickened. "Yes, it is."

"I know it's Valentine's day, but you don't need to drop all of your raise on me." Merrick shifted in his seat, the discomfort clear on his handsome face.

Arching a brow, Toby let a sly smile pull across his lips. "Maybe I'm wooing you."

With a blink, Merrick chuckled as he sat back. "You've already got me."

Toby signaled the waiter. "Not entirely," he murmured, being purposely mysterious.

The man returned to their table carrying a bouquet of long-stemmed, red roses with a card attached and handed the flowers to Merrick.

"These are beautiful." He grinned at Toby. "How very romantic of you."

Toby nodded at the bouquet. "Open the card." He fished in his pocket for the box while Merrick concentrated on opening the envelope, pushing up the seal with his finger, and lifting the small, pale-pink paper. Popping open the box, Toby waited for Merrick to look up.

"Be mine?" His boyfriend's eyes widened as his gaze shot from the note to the box in Toby's hand. "Oh, my God."

Nerves fluttered in Toby's chest. "Is that a yes?" he asked breathlessly, afraid to smile.

"I *am* yours." Merrick's voice caught, and his eyes glittered in the candlelight.

He had to be sure, needing to hear the simple, one-word response. "But now, you'll be mine forever?"

Without an ounce of hesitation, Merrick nodded. "Yes."

Toby gave the waiter a thumbs-up and returned his attention to Merrick, pulling the ring from the box and taking his fiancé's hand. He slipped the gold ring, inset with fourteen small diamonds, onto Merrick's finger.

Merrick's voice caught as he stared at their hands. "It's beautiful."

"Not as beautiful as you are." Toby released his grip on Merrick's hand when the waiter returned with two flutes of prosecco. He set the glasses in front of the two men and retreated wordlessly, though with a warm smile.

Raising his flute, Toby locked his lover in his gaze. "Merrick, you came into my life at one of my lowest points and didn't give up on me, even when I pushed you away. This last year has been amazing, and I love you deeply."

Merrick lifted his glass and touched it to Toby's. "I love you, too."

They sipped the prosecco, and Toby cleared his throat as he set the wine back onto the table. "I was thinking, you could move into my apartment while we house-hunt."

Both eyebrows shot up as Merrick set his own glass on the table. "House-hunt?"

"With the raise and the bonus, I can afford a mortgage. I've also been setting aside quite a bit of my salary the last six months for the up-front money." He wriggled his eyebrows. "I even have enough for a quick wedding and a kickass party."

Merrick laughed. "I'm looking forward to that." He grew serious. "But, Toby, we're entering into a partnership. I fully expect to pull my weight."

"Of course." He took another sip of the bubbly. "I think you should finish your degree. You're too smart and industrious to be a career concierge."

Merrick wrinkled his nose. "Funny you should mention that. I was going to tell you yesterday that I got a call from an Amazon headhunter." He smiled easily as he settled back on his chair. "You distracted me, though, by pouncing and ravaging me when I came over after work."

Toby chuckled. "Can you blame me? You're adorable, and I hadn't seen you in ten whole hours."

"Oh, I didn't mind. Anyway, I have an interview on Friday." He frowned. "I'm sorry I can't be away the whole week with you."

Leaning forward, Toby held out his hand and relished the touch when Merrick took it. "Beautiful man, you just accepted my marriage proposal. We have the rest of our lives to spend together."

Did you enjoy *I'm Yours*?
If so, check out *The Wedding Weekend*,
Book Four of the Rain City.

ALSO BY BRENT ARCHER

Rain City Tales

The Officer's Siren (Book 1)
Past Secrets Present Danger (Book 2)
I'm Yours (Book 3)
The Wedding Weekend (Book 4)
Mitch's Men (Book 4.5)
Saving Parker (Book 5)
Song of Salvation (Book 6)
Memories of Coromandel (Book 7)
Blaze of Cortez (Book 8) – Coming in 2024

Black Rock Cult Series

Rediscovering Todd (Book 1)
Hiding Hayden (Book 2) – Coming in 2024
Dragging Marshall (Book 3) – Coming in 2025

Stand-Alone Stories

Throuple Honey

ABOUT THE AUTHOR

Brent Archer was born in Spokane, Washington, and lived there most of his adolescent life. At 18, he left for Seattle to attend the University of Washington for Electrical Engineering. Quickly, it became apparent that he wasn't wired for the required science and differential equation classes, and so he switched his major to International Studies with a minor in History. After graduation, he pursued an acting career in musical theater and dance. Once thirty hit, however, he decided to focus on numbers, getting a certificate in accounting, and became the Financial Controller of a non-profit arts and music organization.

Though writing most of his life, he never thought to submit his work for publication. In 2012, he visited his cousin Delilah Devlin in Arkansas, and she prodded him to write a story and submit it. So, he did, and it sold right away. With the encouragement of Delilah, his other writing cousin Elle James, and his husband, Brent embarked on a writing career. He's loving the journey, finding inspiration and a story everywhere he goes, whether it be the local coffee shop, driving through each of the United States, or riding the train to explore the world.

www.ingramcontent.com/pod-product-compliance
Lightning Source LLC
Chambersburg PA
CBHW060114260626
47160CB00005B/1886